ISOLATION

Look for other REMNANTS™
titles by K.A. Applegate:

#1 The Mayflower Project

#2 Destination Unknown

#3 Them

#4 Nowhere Land

#5 Mutation

#6 Breakdown

Also by K.A. Applegate

ANIMORPHS®

REMNANTS

ISOLATION

K.A. APPLEGATE

AN
APPLE
PAPERBACK

SCHOLASTIC INC.
New York Toronto London Auckland Sydney
Mexico City New Delhi Hong Kong Buenos Aires

ISBN 0-590-88196-5

12 11 10 9 8 7 6 5 4 3 2 1   2 3 4 5 6 7/0

Printed in the U.S.A.   40
First Scholastic printing, July 2002

For Michael and Jake

ISOLATION

(CHAPTER ONE)

"WE ARE ON THE PATH."

Yago was glad to be alive. Glad to look out over the coppery ocean glittering on his left. Glad to scan the forest of slender, pliant trees on his right for enemies.

He had many enemies. Riders. Blue Meanies. Squids. And the other group of human Remnants, the freaks and their protectors. But so what? The important thing was that he was still alive.

Alive when he should have been dead.

He'd been hooked up to Mother, the highly advanced computer that ran this spaceship. Mother had absorbed the contents of his brain — every memory, fear, secret, and hope — in a heartbeat. Then she'd made him face dark terrors, including his own death in a terrible, desperate battle. The horror of it should have killed him or made him go nuts. But he was still alive, still sane.

There could be only one explanation.

He was the One.

Anyone could see it with one quick glance. Yago was tall and powerfully built. His hair was a lovely leaf green. His eyes were a distinct reflective golden color derived from cat DNA. His teeth were straight and perfectly white. His skin, a glowing bronze.

In short, Yago was beautiful. Whole. Pure.

The One.

Everything made sense now. The asteroid that destroyed Earth five hundred years earlier wasn't a result of random chance or cosmic bad luck or Mother Nature run amok. The asteroid was part of a plan to set humanity on a new path, the path of purity.

Purity.

The word burned in Yago's brain. He loved it, felt he had always loved it. He repeated it to himself with every step he took behind Tamara and the Baby. Purity. Purity. Purity.

Seven billion people had lived on Earth in 2011, the Year of Impact. Of those billions, only eighty were lucky enough to board the *Mayflower,* a space shuttle fitted out with experimental solar sails and experimental hibernation equipment.

Nobody had expected the *Mayflower Project* to succeed. The antique shuttle had no destination, no goal. NASA scientists had merely fired it into space and hoped it would arrive somewhere safe *and* in one piece.

Many of the original Eighty died on the voyage. Some molded and turned to "cheese." Carnivorous worms ate others. Some slowly dried out until they resembled mummies. And the rest had tiny holes drilled into them by micrometeorites.

The *Mayflower* had not landed on a planet, as some optimists had hoped, but on a vast and advanced ship. Those who survived the journey woke to find themselves in a strange environment based on the work of artists long dead and best forgotten.

Why?

Yago didn't know and he really didn't care.

He did know the environments were often deadly and that they were made deadlier by three alien species that seemed determined to take control of Mother.

Some of the Wakers had died since they landed. Riders wiped out Errol. Wylson Lefkowitz-Blake drowned. Blue Meanie fléchette gunfire shredded Shy Hwang. And there were others among the dead: Big Bill, Alberto, and the doctor.

Just nineteen people survived. A ridiculous, laughably small subset of humanity.

And among those remaining nineteen, distinctions could be drawn. *Should* be drawn. At least according to Yago. Not all of them were chosen. Not all of them were pure enough to follow the path.

Some were freaks. 2Face, with her burned flesh. Edward, a human chameleon. Violet Blake, who had lost a finger to the worms. Billy Weir, with his unnatural telepathic abilities. Kubrick, who Mother had skinned in a botched attempt to make him look more like her creators.

The freaks' protectors — Mo'Steel and Jobs — also could not be saved. Yago knew the truth. Those who sought to protect the freaks were as bad as the freaks themselves.

They were not chosen.

And then there were Tamara and the Baby. They were evil, a powerful evil that existed to test Yago's worthiness as the One. Yago was not afraid of them. He would turn them to his own uses. He would allow Tamara to take out as many of the Riders and Squids and Blue Meanies and freaks as possible. Every enemy she killed would bring him closer to controlling the ship. Once he controlled the ship, he would lead his followers in building a paradise.

Yago's gaze fell on D-Caf and Anamull, walking a few steps ahead of him. He smiled.

Anamull was a big kid. He was quiet, withdrawn, blank. Yago thought of him as a follower, a soldier.

D-Caf was more complicated. He was a toady in training. A twitch hiding behind his stooped posture and idiotic jokes. But Yago saw something in his eyes. A quiet watchfulness. Yago was certain D-Caf wasn't as stupid as he seemed.

Yago jogged up and fell into step with the other guys, ready to begin enlightening them. "We are on the path," he announced.

Anamull sent him a guarded glance. "You know where we're going? Because I'm getting a little tired of following after Tamara and her, um, Baby."

"Forget about Tamara," Yago said impatiently. "She is only my tool. I'm telling you that soon our enemies will fall and the One will rule. We are on the path."

D-Caf smiled uncertainly. *"The One?"* he asked.

"All those who are pure are chosen," Yago said.

Anamull and D-Caf stared back at him with expressions of complete confusion. Yago felt like reaching out and slapping the ignorant looks off their faces. *Patience,* he told himself. It had taken him fifteen years, or five hundred and fifteen years, to see the path. Simple soldiers must be given time to understand.

"Hey, everyone! Look!"

The kid. Roger Dodger. He was yelling and pointing at the sky. Tamara stopped. The rest of the group stopped behind her. The Baby turned its empty eye sockets toward the sky as if it could actually see.

Two Squids were flying by, passing in the opposite direction from the way the Remnants were marching. They passed high overhead, bodies thrust forward, tentacle arms waving.

Yago waited patiently. Let Tamara figure out what the Squids were up to. Let her decimate them all. That was what he was waiting for.

All he needed was time.

All he needed was patience.

They were on the path.

(CHAPTER TWO)

"WHERE ARE WE GOING, ANYWAY?"

Jobs had never been a nature lover, and he hated this marsh. He hated having wet feet. He hated climbing up and down the endless rolling hills.

He kept flashing on the old war movies his grandfather used to watch late at night: bad guys concealed under the water, land mines exploding, good guys bleeding and dying.

"Cheer up, Duck!" Mo'Steel said, putting an arm around Jobs's shoulder. "Things could be worse."

Jobs nodded without smiling. Things *had* been worse. Recently and often. At least there was no sign of the Riders. At least he knew his little brother, Edward, was safe. He was just a few yards ahead, walking with 2Face and Kubrick. Jobs tried not to focus on how his little brother's skin was becoming the same color as the warm copper-colored water they were wading through.

"I just don't see the point of sloshing around in this swamp," Jobs said. "Where are we going, anyway?"

"We're following 2Face," Mo'Steel said.

"Well, at least we know she's happy," Jobs said petulantly. For some reason he couldn't understand, 2Face was determined to be in charge. Had been ever since they woke up on the shuttle. She'd forced them to choose between following Tamara and the Baby and following her.

Jobs knew 2Face was right to fear the Baby. The Baby creeped him out, too. Creeped everyone out. But he thought the Remnants had enough problems without breaking into factions. And he couldn't really blame the people who had decided to follow Tamara.

Tamara had promised them the Baby would turn the ship into a re-creation of good old Earth. Wanting to go home again was only natural, only human. If Jobs had believed Tamara could deliver on her promise, he would have joined her himself. But he knew that what she was offering was impossible.

"Would you prefer if someone else was in charge?" Noyze asked quietly.

Noyze and Dr. Cohen had only just joined the other Remnants. While Jobs, Mo'Steel, and the others had been dealing with the Tower of Babel and fighting the British from the U.S.S. *Constitution,* they'd been prisoners of the Blue Meanies. Jobs realized Noyze and Dr. Cohen were still getting to know their new companions, still trying to figure out who to trust.

Even now, Dr. Cohen was walking with Mo'Steel's mother and asking her a thousand questions. They were so intent on their conversation that they kept falling behind. Not exactly safe under the circumstances.

"No," Jobs said. "I mean, I don't know. I just wish we were heading somewhere instead of splashing around."

"Where do you want to go?" Violet Blake asked.

"To the bridge," Jobs said.

Finding the bridge was the key to controlling the ship, the key to their survival. And Jobs had an almost physical need to **see** the machine that had created the strange environments they'd endured. He needed to understand it.

"We go to the bridge and we'll probably get involved in a big shootout." Mo'Steel didn't sound afraid and Jobs knew he wasn't. Mo liked action, even action of the most desperate and dangerous sort.

"The surviving Blue Meanies will probably head there," Noyze said.

"Tamara, too," Mo'Steel said.

"Maybe we should double back and follow Tamara," Violet suggested. "If we're lucky, she'll lead us to the bridge."

"Tamara is not heading toward the bridge," Billy said, speaking for the first time. He'd been there all along, of course, trudging silently between Violet and Mo'Steel. Still, Jobs was surprised whenever he heard his voice. Billy had been silent and catatonic for so long that hearing him speak was a little like being addressed by a park bench.

"How do you know?" Noyze tended to treat Billy like just another kid. Jobs had told her that Billy had some strange abilities, but she hadn't been around long enough to witness them.

"I can . . . sense . . . her mind," Billy tried to explain.

Jobs was impatient to hear more. "So where is she going?" he asked eagerly.

"I don't know," Billy said. "I can't really get ahold of her thoughts. There are lots of colors. I see determination, anger."

"Her determination or the Baby's?" Violet asked.

"I don't know," Billy said. "It's impossible for me to separate the two."

Violet shuddered. "I wonder if Tamara is the Baby's partner or its slave?"

"Slave," Mo'Steel said with conviction. "I don't know about the rest of you, but the Baby gives me the allover creepy crawlies. If we let it take control of the ship, I predict something very, very nasty is going to happen."

"How can we stop it?" Noyze asked.

"Take control ourselves," Mo'Steel said.

Noyze laughed, but quickly caught herself when she realized Mo'Steel and the others were serious. "Could we really do that?"

"It's a long shot," Jobs said thoughtfully. "But Mother seems weaker after her encounter with Alberto. Now may be our best chance."

"Squids!" Edward yelled.

"Take cover!" 2Face ordered.

Jobs crouched down, hiding himself as well as he could in the tall grass. His skin was clammy, heart racing. The Squids — about a dozen of them — were flying overhead.

Jobs cautiously looked up, his heart in his throat. The Squids seemed to be flying randomly. Circling, as if they were searching for something. Then —

A few of the Squids rocketed down toward the

surface. Ahead of him! The Squids were going to land ahead of him. They were going to get Edward!

No!

Jobs was on his feet, running, sliding on the silty mud and slippery grass. He reached Edward. Tackled him from behind. Covered him with his own body.

"Hey — quit it!" Edward yelled, outraged. "What are you doing? Let me go!"

By then, Jobs had seen his mistake. The Squids weren't attacking Edward. They were coming down farther, just ahead of them.

Mo'Steel ran past, keeping his footing with no trouble, charging up the hill. Jobs released Edward and followed. He was wet, out of breath, and scared by the time he reached Mo'Steel at the top of the hill.

And on top of the very next hill was a Blue Meanie.

The Squids had landed near it, but the Blue Meanie wasn't paying much attention to them. Jobs got the impression it was intent on whatever it was doing.

Blue Meanies went everywhere, wearing space suits that doubled as body armor. Their bodies were roughly pony-shaped and pony-sized. They had four legs tapering down and ending without apparent feet and eyes on either side of a low-slung head.

But there the similarity to any Earth creature ended. Two serpentine tentacles moved on each side of this Blue Meanie's head. Jobs had seen the Blue Meanies use their tentacles to communicate, but this one seemed to have them attached to something under the grass. While the Remnants watched, it pulled out a piece of metal.

"What's it doing?" Jobs asked.

"Don't know," Mo'Steel said. "Hull repairs?"

"We better go around it," Jobs said. He turned to face the others, who were still trudging up the hill.

"Whoa!" Mo'Steel yelled.

Jobs spun in time to see two of the Squids' blasting matter jets hit the Blue Meanie in the chest. The Meanie exploded in a blaze of red light.

The others came at a run. "What just happened?" 2Face asked.

"The Squids wasted a Blue Meanie," Mo'Steel said.

"Strange," Jobs said. "When we saw the Squids and Meanies fighting over the statue, the Squids seemed totally outgunned. This time, they destroyed the Meanie with one shot."

"They are in active mode," Billy said.

"Meaning what, exactly?" Olga asked.

"The Squids are Mother's security system," Billy explained. "She programmed them to attack anyone who tries to harm her when she is defenseless. Their job is to keep her safe while she rebuilds."

"Programmed them?" Violet asked. "Aren't they alive?"

"No," Billy said. "They're automatons."

"Living machines," Jobs said.

"That's pretty horrible," Violet said, her pretty features filled with disgust.

Jobs didn't think it was horrible. The concept of biological machines had always fascinated him. Scientists on Earth hadn't advanced the field beyond the most preliminary of experiments — and even that had raised the ire of moralists and the United States Congress.

Jobs suddenly found himself much more interested in the Squids. Still, he had to admit, the challenge of controlling the ship had just gotten much harder.

If the Squids could take out a Blue Meanie, humans would definitely be easy picking.

CHAPTER THREE

"YOU WILL WAIT."

Tamara didn't waste a minute.

As soon as 2Face made her little speech and the Remnants chose sides, Tamara had simply headed off without a word of explanation. She left the others to follow as best they could.

Tate tried to keep up with Tamara.

Easier said than done.

Within five minutes, Tate was sweating. Ten more minutes, and her lungs and thighs were burning. Before half an hour had passed, she longed to plop down on the strange beach and take a nap. But Tamara never slowed, never rested. She carried her hideous, overgrown Baby effortlessly on one slim hip and just kept moving.

Matching her pace was exhausting, but nobody complained. Nobody even spoke. They were afraid. Tate could feel the tension in the air, could see it in the way the others kept their eyes down and their questions to themselves.

The air was damp. Humid as a Florida swamp on an August evening. Their footsteps kicked up something friable like black peat moss that covered the shore of the copper-colored sea. The dust clung to Tate's sticky legs, worked its way into her shoes, made her skin itch. Still, she refused to fall behind.

Tate had wanted to join 2Face, Olga, Jobs, and Mo'Steel. She would have even put up with that insipid superfemme, Violet Blake. 2Face's group was more tolerant. More moral, as silly as that sounded.

Tamara's group couldn't have been more different.

Yago was a bigot. Prejudiced against everyone except his own silver-spoon-sucking self. Tate had never liked him or his kiss-my-feet attitude, but he'd been quieter since he'd connected with Mother. At first, Tate had thought he was embarrassed after having Mother parade all of his petty little fantasies in front of everyone.

But no. Something about Yago's eyes was very wrong. Something about the strange, beatific smile he wore as he trudged along. He was planning something. Something disturbing.

And the Baby. They were so afraid of the Baby

that they couldn't see it was playing with them, testing to see how far they would go.

Tate felt as if she'd stepped voluntarily into a hornet's nest.

But she had no choice.

She had to protect Tamara.

She had no idea why. But she was driven.

Tate had to save her from the Baby. She knew she wasn't strong enough to defeat it by herself. So she was going to try and remind Tamara of her own humanity, to encourage her to resist.

Without warning, Tamara stopped and put the Baby down. "We'll rest here," she announced.

Groaning with relief, everyone sat wherever they were standing. Roger Dodger immediately took off his shoes, went down to the water, and got his feet wet.

Joining him on the shore, Tate sank down to her knees and drank the silty, lukewarm water. Not exactly refreshing, but it hadn't made them sick yet. Of course, there was nothing to eat. But hunger wasn't so bad. Not when you compared it to thirst.

Tate watched Tamara for a few minutes. She was crouching in the strange soil, her expression blank. The Baby was nearby, gazing off in the direction they were heading. An imposing duo. Still, Tate gathered her resolve and approached Tamara.

"Weird landscape," she said, aiming for a casual tone.

Tamara stared. The Baby turned its eyeless sockets toward Tate and bared tiny white teeth that somehow managed to be threatening. Tate could feel the others watching her from behind. She was breaking an unspoken taboo. Nobody ever talked to Tamara unless they were up to their armpits in Riders.

"So, where are you from? I mean — back when we still had a planet?" Tate asked.

Tamara continued to stare. Then she blinked slowly and nodded. "Tennessee."

Tate went blank for a moment. Then she forced herself to relax.

"I've never been to Tennessee," Tate admitted. "But my family went to North Carolina on vacation once. Outer Banks. The beach there was pretty nice — nicer than this one anyway. Have you ever been there?"

"No," Tamara said.

This wasn't going to be easy. But Tate realized the Baby had looked away, dismissed her. Tamara seemed to relax, soften.

"I was supposed to go to Myrtle Beach on my honeymoon," Tamara said, almost dreamily. "We never did get to go. Steve and I could never get leave at the same time."

Tamara was talking. Good sign.

"Seafood," Tate said. "I don't know about Myrtle Beach, but the seafood was amazing on the Outer Banks. Shrimp. Great shrimp."

"Most seafood gives me hives," Tamara said. She looked at Tate with an expression that was scared and haunted and human. Tate's pulse raced. Tamara was still in there. Tate could almost believe she was asking for help.

Before Tate could fashion a reply, Tamara rose gracefully to her feet and picked up the Baby. "There's a Rider outpost up ahead," she announced to the entire group. "You will stay behind while I go scout the situation."

"How long will that take?" Burroway demanded.

"You will wait," Tamara said.

"You can't just leave us sitting here, out in the open, defenseless," Burroway insisted.

"You will wait," Tamara repeated.

Tate thought she saw something in Tamara's eyes. Was it fear? Was the Baby getting her into a situation she couldn't handle? Tate had seen Tamara battle the Riders back at the Tower of Babel. Tamara had fought bravely. With more than human speed and strength. She'd taken out six Riders.

But this was different. The Baby was leading Tamara into a Rider camp. Who knew how many Riders would be there? A dozen? Two dozen? More?

Even Tamara had her limits.

She deserved some backup.

Tate made her decision.

She waited until Tamara had walked off and the others were busy trying to get as comfortable as possible on the open ground. Then she wandered casually to the line of strange trees that tossed in a breeze Tate couldn't even feel. She stepped gingerly in among their roots. Nobody noticed, or if they did, they didn't say anything. Maybe they assumed she was going to pee.

The tree roots rose up out of the ground almost like mangrove roots, creating an obstacle course around Tate's ankles. Climbing over them was going to be hard work.

Tate didn't have a moment to waste. She would have to move fast if she wanted to keep up with Tamara.

And the Baby.

(CHAPTER FOUR)

"YOUR MAKER IS NO FOOL."

Tate's eyes skimmed the ground for her next step. On top of a tree root. Between two big ones. Jogging, almost hopping, clinging to branches, swinging herself forward. Careful of the ankles. Tate didn't want to break any bones. Not here, beyond any hope of medical care.

As often as she dared, Tate looked up to verify that Tamara was still there, walking down the beach with the Baby on her hip. Mostly, Tate kept her eyes on her feet.

She didn't notice the bones at first. When she first started to see one here and one there, she thought they were tree roots or downed branches.

But, after a while, there were so many that she couldn't ignore them. Slender, delicate bones scattered over the ground almost like pine needles. Tate guessed they came from the eel-like fish that swam in the copper-colored sea. There was also an occasional pointy-nosed skull that could have belonged to a rodent of some sort.

And then a sight that made her gasp and stop. A skeleton. What had to be a Rider skeleton latched up into the branches of a tree. The tree's swaying motion moved the skeleton slowly back and forth in front of Tate's face as if it were taunting her.

A spine somehow supporting two skulls. The first, the most noticeable, was a simple cylinder rimmed with razor-sharp teeth. The other was much like a human skull except that there were too many openings for too many eyes. Arm bones. Hand bones. No ribs. But legs, knees, hips, feet.

At the base of the tree trunk was one of the Riders' hoverboards. It was broken into two perfect halves. The arced pieces were stuck down into the soil so they formed a V. Between the V sat one of the curved spears the Riders used in battle. The blade had also been broken in half.

Tate knelt down and picked up the two pieces of the spear. The top piece was maybe a foot long — a shard of razor-sharp blade. Tate didn't see how she could carry it without the risk of slicing herself to pieces. But the bottom piece still had the hilt attached. Tate hooked the hilt through her belt and let the two-foot-long blade hang loose.

When Tate got back to her feet, Tamara had disappeared. Tate started to carefully run through the roots. Then she realized there wasn't much point in staying under the cover of the trees if Tamara couldn't see her. She crossed back out onto the beach and started to run at full speed.

The thickness of the air slowed her down a bit. It was filled with wood smoke, frying fat, and something she couldn't identify. Then she saw the camp.

The Riders had built about a dozen structures right on the line where the woods met the beach. The buildings were up on stilts that were about as tall as Tate. On top of the stilts sat simple wooden platforms. The sides of the structures were open but the Riders had thatched simple roofs out of the yellow grasses.

Down on the beach was a ring of charred ground, big enough for twenty or thirty Riders to stand around. As Tate watched, Tamara stepped into the middle of the ring and put the Baby down at her feet.

The reaction was immediate.

An unearthly chorus like a factory full of metal wheels grinding together. Tate couldn't see even a single Rider, but she heard their reaction to Tamara and the Baby.

A Rider came zooming in on his hoverboard, accelerating toward Tamara.

Tamara stood waiting.

The Rider stopped at the edge of the ring and swung at Tamara with a spear.

Tamara reacted almost casually. She bent her knees to avoid the blow. As she stood, she swung her right hand back, caught the blade on the dull outside, and wrenched it away from the Rider.

In one fluid motion, she switched the hilt to her left hand, leaped forward. The Rider fell forward, his board careening wildly off toward the water.

He fell and was very still.

Tamara retrieved the spear and spoke. "I will speak to the leader of the Clan," she said in a voice that Tate heard clearly.

Another Rider appeared from under the trees. Unlike the first challenger, he moved slowly and with grace. He was missing one "arm" and his carapace was dull and scarred. But he did not hesitate as he approached the edge of the ring.

"You will bring it to me," Tamara said.

A calm clicking response from the Rider. Tate had no way of knowing what he was saying.

"The species that calls itself the Children. Do not toy with me. Your Maker is no fool. Bring the one you have to me *immediately* or perish."

This time the leader made no spoken response.

Two Riders appeared on foot. They hopped forward strangely, using swords to force a Blue Meanie to walk between them. The Blue Meanie was stumbling from exhaustion or wounds or fear. His midnight-colored space suit was dinged and scratched from battle.

Tamara tore off the Blue Meanie's suit.

Tate gasped. Without its suit the Blue Meanie was far smaller than she would have expected. The body was delicate, with spindly legs and two large, dark eyes. But the creature's flesh was weird — bare and wrinkled and rubbery-looking, like something pulled from a moist and dark cave.

Tamara lowered the Baby toward the Blue Meanie. The Baby cackled in glee and clapped its little hands. Then it reached out and touched the Blue Meanie with one hand.

Tate watched in horror as the Baby's brown skin darkened, then flushed red. The red brightened and extended beyond the Baby's body like a radioactive glow.

The Blue Meanie's tentacles waved wildly in the

air. Its legs and head went stiff and trembled. Then the alien's body seemed to suddenly dissolve.

Somehow, the Baby seemed to absorb it. But not through its nose or mouth. The Blue Meanie just disappeared without a trace.

Suddenly, the Baby began to expand. Its skin faded until it was translucent except for the skin of its now cone-shaped head. That was opaque and quivering.

Shipwright, Tate told herself.

She'd heard 2Face accuse the Baby of being a Shipwright back when 2Face had insisted they all get far, far away from the Baby. But somehow she hadn't imagined such a terrifying and complete transformation.

"You know that I am your Maker, one of the Guardians of the past," the Baby/Shipwright said. A wavering, watery voice devoid of emotion. Tate was surprised the alien could talk. It had no mouth.

She was even more surprised she could understand what it was saying.

(CHAPTER FIVE)

AREN'T WE MISSING SOMEONE?

The Clan did not fear the gods.

The Clan did not fear the Makers.

Varchazertak Badad-Varchazer, warrior of the Bonilivak Clan, listened.

"Your people were created by mine and you are forever indebted," the human-not-human said. "We gave you power and strength, and in return you fought for us. Now you must fight for your Makers again."

Like the other members of the Clan, Varchazertak Badad-Varchazer waited silently. It was proper for the herald, Sincomantak Badad-Sincoman, to reply.

"We do not fear death," Sincomantak Badad-Sincoman said.

"We do not fear death," Varchazertak Badad-Varchazer echoed along with the rest of the Clan.

"So you will fight?" the human-not-human demanded. The other was quiet now, although the arc between the two glowed strongly and bright.

"We will not fight," Sincomantak Badad-Sincoman said even as his eating head snapped greedily.

"Explain yourself!" roared the human-not-human.

Some of the Clan also vocalized. Sincomantak Badad-Sincoman's decision would not be popular in the Clan Council. The newest warriors were anxious to go into battle against the invaders and earn whatever glory the gods had chosen for them. Many would challenge Sincomantak Badad-Sincoman's leadership. So it had always been.

"We call you *not* our Maker," Sincomantak Badad-Sincoman said calmly. "Our Makers disappeared when many who are Sanctified Ancestors were few-deaths. We ruled ourselves for a very long time. We do not need Makers anymore. We do not want them."

"I challenge your leadership," the human-not-human said.

"This is not the way things can work," Sincomantak Badad-Sincoman said. "Only Clan members can challenge my leadership. You are not a member. You have not bled for a place in the Clan Council."

"I have! In the old days, members of the Clan followed the Rule of Nine."

"The Bonilivak Clan still follows the Rule of Nine," Sincomantak Badad-Sincoman said strongly.

So it was. Any Clan member who wished to be herald had to fight nine opponents, one after another. Many had fought and beaten seven. Not so many had fought and beaten eight. But Sincomantak Badad-Sincoman was always the ninth opponent. None had ever beaten him.

"I offer a new Rule of Nine," the unhuman-calls-itself-Maker said. "The human-not-human will fight nine members of the Clan at the same time. If she wins, you will make her leader of the Clan."

"Oh, no," Tate muttered to herself. "Oh, this is *so* not good."

She hadn't understood a thing the Riders had said. But she'd heard the Baby say Tamara, the "human-not-human," would fight nine Riders at the same time. And she could see the Riders gathering, their weapons shimmering dimly in the misty light. Nine against one? Crazy. Impossible.

Eight Riders got into position. One stood directly in front of Tamara while the others formed a semicircle behind him.

Aren't we missing someone? Tate wondered. The Baby had said Tamara would fight nine Riders. Why were only eight in position?

Tamara stood waiting, looking sure of herself even as the Baby crawled out of the circle. She reached down, almost casually, and picked up the fallen guard's scimitar.

Tate drew the partial sword out of her belt loop and swallowed down the foul-tasting bile that was rising in her throat. She began to move slowly through the trees, closer to the circle.

The first Rider surged forward. His hoverboard was waist-high on Tamara. He closed in — five feet, three feet, one foot. Tamara shoved the scimitar deep into the loose soil. She kicked her right leg and hit the leading edge of the board.

The Rider fell forward, neatly impaling himself on Tamara's weapon.

One down.

The Baby clapped and giggled.

But now the others were closing in. Two — no, three! — swords aimed at Tamara's head, chest, legs.

Tamara dropped flat onto her stomach. She rolled, pulling the dead guard on top of her, using him as a shield.

One of the Riders followed through with his sword and buried the edge into the chest of another Rider, who howled in pain and swerved off.

The third Rider moved in, awkwardly trying to attack Tamara while balancing on his board. Tamara grabbed the leading edge of his sword and thrust it back with incredible force. He dropped his weapon.

Tamara hopped to her feet. She grabbed the weapon, leaped onto the hoverboard.

"You go, girl," Tate whispered.

Blood was dripping from Tamara's right hand. She kicked the Rider's body off the hoverboard, ducked to avoid an incoming boomerang, and then —

Fast! A blur of speed and Tamara zoomed out over the sea. Tate had never seen a hoverboard move so fast. Six Riders followed, but they were much slower.

Another injured Rider lagged farther and farther behind, his hoverboard slowing like a toy whose batteries were running low. The hoverboard slipped into the water, still carrying the Rider.

Tamara could have easily outrun the Riders, but she stopped a hundred feet from the shore, waiting for the fastest to get close. She leaped twice her height, did a midair somersault, and landed on his board. The two went over into the water.

Tate could see splashing and hear the Rider shrieking. Once, twice, the Rider's eating head came up, but Tate didn't see Tamara. The splashing quieted quickly. Tate scanned the water, anxious to see who would come up for air.

The remaining four Riders seemed to be doing the same. They circled around the area, stabbing randomly at the water.

No sign of the Rider. No sign of Tamara.

Then —

A flash! Something flying out of the water. A boomerang! It spun through the air and lodged itself in one of the Riders.

The stricken Rider quickly slowed his board and reached back. His four-fingered hand found the weapon. And he pulled it free. The Rider slumped to one side, dead or unconscious, his hoverboard careening off to sea.

A beat. Another beat. Another.

Still no Tamara.

How long had gone by? Two minutes? Three? Tate had no idea, but she knew it was much longer than a human could live without breathing.

One of the Riders was acting strangely. He was surfing along carefully, spear at the ready, clearly following the movement of something under the water. Tamara. It had to be. And she couldn't come up for air without the risk of being speared like a fish.

The two other Riders lined up behind the first. The Baby wasn't laughing now.

Riders were good at catching fish. Tate knew that from the bones that filled the forest.

Silence.

Then a squeal painful in its intensity. One of the Riders pulled up a gasping, sputtering Tamara from the water, his spear poking through the seat of her pants. Maybe poking through her skin, too. Tate couldn't tell.

Another Rider reached down and pulled Tamara up by her close-cropped hair.

Big mistake.

Tamara swung up and landed her heels directly in the Rider's insect eyes.

The Rider didn't let go. He reached for his spear. But he was too close to use it. Tamara's hands, feet, elbows, and knees flew as she landed dozens of superfast punches on his eyes and weak, wailing mouth. His eating mouth grinded greedily, anticipating the kill.

Another Rider let loose a boomerang. It *fwop-fwopped* toward Tamara's lower back. Tamara pushed off against her capturer's carapace and did a midair headstand. The boomerang hit her capturer in the torso.

Now free, Tamara crouched on the hoverboard, grabbed the spear the Rider was still clutching in his hand, and threw it left-handed toward one of the remaining Riders. Direct hit.

One Rider remained. He fled, back toward land and the outpost. Tamara followed, catching up as easily as a Porsche chasing a bicycle. She threw the boomerang. The Rider zigzagged as he reached the beach. Miss! The boomerang turned, started back toward Tamara. The Rider zagzigged. The boomerang grazed his leg but didn't stop him.

Tamara leaped, landing with her arms around the Rider's shoulders. One swift move and the Rider was down.

But Tamara looked almost as bad. She crouched on the hoverboard, arms hanging limply at her side, hand bleeding, clothes dripping, eyes closed, obviously beyond exhausted.

That's when her ninth opponent revealed himself.

(CHAPTER SIX)

"STAND IN THE MAKER'S WAY AND DIE."

Tate instantly recognized him as the Rider Tamara and the Baby had been speaking with. Something about him was different from the other Riders — more intimidating.

His hoverboard bore a series of small blue daubs attached to the leading edge. His carapace, arms, and legs were speckled with scars that were a lighter rust color than the rest of his body. Hundreds of shiny white teeth decorated his bandolier.

His fancy attire and battered appearance made Tate guess he was some sort of leader. As he regally rode his hoverboard toward Tamara, a deafening shrieking rose from the woods. Tate looked around fearfully. Clearly, the woods were full of Riders. She would never escape if Tamara lost this fight.

Tamara brought her head up like a person emerging from a coma. Groggily, she watched the chief Rider approach. The Baby bared its teeth and stared at him with its eyeless sockets.

From the chief Rider's bandolier hung boomerangs and a short spear. He carried a scimitar, poised to strike.

Tamara had no weapons.

Oh, this is fair, Tate thought angrily. Of course, the whole thing had been unfair from the beginning.

Now an eerie calm fell over the scene. Tate could almost feel the Riders' intensity, willing their chief to prevail.

The chief Rider threw a boomerang, followed by another, another, and another. Tate followed their spinning, speeding trajectories. One was heading directly toward Tamara's face, another to her right, another to her left, and another slightly above her head.

Diving from her hoverboard, Tamara hit the dust and rolled. The chief Rider was instantly on her, jabbing with his spear, aiming for her eyes, her heart.

Tamara moved with superhuman speed, avoiding the spear by inches, fractions of inches. She had no way to get up, no way to fight back.

Tate fingered the hilt of her sword. Should she get into the fight?

Tate quickly made her decision. She ran out of the woods. "Tamara — take this!"

Tamara saw her, saw the broken sword she was offering. She held out a hand, nodded wearily.

Tate tossed the sword.

The Rider was still busy with his spear.

Tamara curled into a ball, protecting most of her vital organs, and somersaulted toward the sword. The Rider landed a stab — near Tamara's shoulder! Another — near her tailbone! Tate saw red ooze stain Tamara's clothing.

But now she had her fingers on the sword. She picked it up and flung it. The sword flipped through the air, unbalanced. The shaft broadsided the Rider in the chest. The impact knocked him off his board.

Before he could sit up, Tamara was on him.

And then, it was over.

Tamara had won.

The Baby smiled.

Tate rushed out of the woods. "Tamara! Tamara, are you okay?"

Tamara shoved Tate aside, picked up the Baby, and addressed the Riders hidden among the trees. "The one you call herald is dead," she said. "The leader of this Clan is now Tamarantak Badad-Tamaran!"

A low clicking from the woods. The Riders slowly revealed themselves. One by one, they approached Tamara and the Baby and laid their scimitars at her feet. The pile grew rapidly until it reached Tate's knees.

Dozens of Riders surrounded them. Hundreds of insect eyes studied them. So many that their strange arid, smoky scent filled Tate's nostrils. Unnerved, she crept closer to Tamara and the Baby.

"Mother has created her own backup security defenses," Tamara said. "They must be destroyed! Those who call themselves Mother's Children still live. They, too, must be destroyed. With their deaths, you will earn back the places you called home. Go. Round up your Clans."

Tate's stomach twisted. She didn't know what she'd been expecting, but it wasn't this. Tamara was declaring war on the Squids and the Blue Meanies! She'd never mentioned this little detail to the Remnants. None of the others knew they were about to be marched into the middle of a war.

"Tamara, wait," Tate said urgently. "Listen. The Blue Meanies have helped us in the past and they've never been our true enemies. Why kill them? Can't we find another way?"

"What do you mean 'our'?" Tamara's eyes were

as flat and unfocused as a doll's. "There is only the Maker. There is only the Maker's will. Only the Maker's needs. Serve the Maker well and live. Stand in the Maker's way and die."

Tate stepped back, suddenly realizing how completely she'd been fooling herself. She couldn't reason with Tamara. Tamara was nothing more than a puppet. And the puppet master wanted war.

Tate turned. Ran! Stumbling at first, then picking up speed. She had to warn the others.

Her back prickled. She expected the bite of Tamara's spear. She expected one of the Riders to run her down. She expected to die at any second.

One yard.

Two.

Three.

Still alive.

CHAPTER SEVEN

"NOW YOU ARE INVOLVED,
AND YOU WILL COMPLY."

D-Caf longed for a book. Any book at all. A comic. A thriller. Some outlandish science-fiction thing. Anything he could prop up in front of his face and block out the rest of the world.

Not being able to read was the second worst thing about this place. The worst thing was the total lack of privacy. D-Caf felt as if he were trapped in a never-ending buddy movie with Yago in the role of his buddy.

They'd been waiting for Tamara to return for two hours, maybe three. D-Caf had spent half of that time in the woods "using the bathroom." But, eventually, he had to come out of the trees and rejoin the others.

Yago was waiting for him.

"We are on the path," Yago whispered, leaning uncomfortably close to D-Caf. His tone was urgent and conspiratorial even though D-Caf had heard this same pronouncement at least a dozen times.

"Good," D-Caf said with all of the enthusiasm he could muster. He could feel Anamull watching them from a dozen yards away. His expression was blank, unreadable.

D-Caf looked for an escape, saw none. Tate had snuck off after Tamara much earlier. Roger Dodger, T.R., and Burroway were lying under the shade of the hyperactive trees, dozing. Jobs or 2Face would have posted a guard, at least. But nobody here seemed to think of it.

"Yes," Yago said with deep satisfaction. "It is good to be chosen. For the Few, great opportunities will arise. Opportunities and struggle. The Few must be willing to work, to sacrifice, to follow. Paradise cannot be built in a day."

"Just like Rome, huh?" D-Caf said with a nervous laugh.

Yago's expression didn't change. "The Few must follow the One," he said. "They must follow without question, without hesitation, without fear."

"Sure," D-Caf agreed. "No problem."

He didn't have to ask who "the One" was. Yago had been acting a tad touched ever since he hooked up with Mother and took them all on a wild ride through Washington, D.C. If their spaceship was going to have a new emperor, Yago's vote was clearly for Yago.

Maybe it's just a mood, D-Caf thought. Mark, his brother and illegal guardian, used to have plenty of moods. Sometimes Mark was the über-parent — packing nutritious lunches for D-Caf, checking his homework, tucking him in at night. Sometimes Mark wouldn't come home for days at a time, claiming he had more important things to do than play house with a kid.

D-Caf had learned to get along with his mercurial older brother. He coped by staying focused on the big picture. For example: Mark's moods were bad, but not as bad as foster care.

Up until now, the big picture said Yago was D-Caf's best hope for survival. Yago needed him.

"Hey, who's that?" D-Caf said, more to change the subject than anything.

It was Tate. She was waving frantically and running down the beach toward them. She stopped down by the water, hands on knees, panting. Everyone rushed to meet her. Clearly, she had something important to say.

"Where have you been?" Burroway demanded. "What happened?"

"Are you all right?" T.R. asked.

Tate nodded urgently, still fighting to control her breath. "I — I thought the Riders were going to kill me. I thought Tamara might — kill me."

"Why would Tamara want to kill you?" Roger Dodger asked. "I thought you were friends."

D-Caf smirked at the kid's question. "Friends," he repeated. "That's a good one."

Nobody else looked amused. D-Caf bit his lower lip.

"I followed her to a Rider outpost," Tate reported. "The Baby is rounding up an army of Riders. They're supposed to kill the Blue Meanies and the Squids and take back the ship for the Baby. It's going to be war and — and I don't know what the Baby has planned for us."

Burroway looked down his beaklike nose at Tate. "I'm sure the Baby doesn't have anything planned for us. We can't fight. We just have to stay out of the way until this blows over. I'll tell Tamara to find us a good place to hide."

"There's a plan," Tate said sarcastically.

"Why? What's wrong with it?" T.R. asked.

"I don't think Tamara can help us," Tate said, almost tearfully. "I saw the Baby absorb a Blue Meanie. The Riders were keeping it hostage. The Baby turned into a Shipwright. When it does that, it's powerful. It doesn't need Tamara. And just think what will happen if there's war. The Baby will have all of the Meanies it needs. It could probably become a Shipwright permanently."

D-Caf looked around the circle. As usual, Yago had a guarded, calculating expression. He was still playing the angles. Anamull was blank as always. Burroway and T.R. seemed lost. Either they didn't get it or they couldn't take it. Roger Dodger was the only one who had the sense to look worried. D-Caf himself was plenty worried, but he did what he could to hide it. Best to lay low until Yago was on the record.

Tate's eyes flittered around the circle and she groaned with frustration. "Let me connect the dots for you. The Baby made an alliance with us. It promised to turn the ship into Earth, right?"

Nods.

"Now the Baby has made an alliance with the Riders," Tate rushed on. "It promised to give them their home back. Anyone see a conflict here?"

"But Tamara said —" Burroway started.

Tate interrupted impatiently. "When Tamara gets back here, if she gets back here, she may be accompanied by a hundred or a thousand Riders. Do you really think she's going to be interested in having a debate with you?"

"What do you mean, 'if'?" Yago asked.

"I think Tamara is in real danger," Tate said. "If the Baby becomes a Shipwright, it won't need her anymore. It could do anything — even kill her."

"Well, that's just beautiful!" Burroway exploded. "Tamara asked us to follow her. We trusted her! And what does she do? Abandons us here with no defenses and sneaks off to make alliances with our enemies. I, for one, am not going to stand for this treatment!"

"Daniel, I think you'd better calm down now," T.R. said.

"Why should I?" Burroway demanded.

T.R. pointed.

Tamara, with the Baby on her back, was surfing toward them on a hoverboard. The group watched silently as she came up behind Burroway. Fifty yards farther behind her, rows of Riders were beginning to line up. D-Caf saw Tate take a step back.

"You all followed me," Tamara said. "I did not force you. Now you are involved, and you will comply."

Tate was right about one thing, D-Caf told himself. *Tamara definitely wasn't interested in a debate.*

CHAPTER EIGHT

"STAY UNDER THE RADAR."

Burroway pointed at Tate. "She said you weren't coming back," he said accusingly. "She said you were selling us out to the Riders. But, but I didn't believe her. And now that you're back, our deal still stands. We'll do whatever you say."

What a weasel, Tate thought. She glanced fearfully at Tamara. Would the Baby kill her as a traitor?

Tamara wasn't looking at Tate. Her eyes were unfocused. She'd wrapped a cloth around her injured hand, and her haggard look was completely gone. In fact, Tate could almost imagine an aura surrounding her. Only this aura didn't have a color; it had a mood, an atmosphere, an ambiance.

An ambiance of evil.

"The Riders are assembling a large army," Tamara informed them. "The Baby will be their leader. They are going to attack those you call Blue

Meanies and Squids. The ones who are guarding the bridge."

Yago was nodding eagerly. The others didn't look particularly concerned.

Tate was amazed. Tamara was organizing an across-the-board massacre of most of the life on the ship and all the others could do was shrug indifferently? Were they completely nuts? And, assuming the answer was yes, weren't they even worried about choosing the wrong side in a war?

"What do you want us to do?" Anamull asked.

"Be quiet and stay out of my way." Tamara's tone was almost mocking, as if she considered them incapable of doing anything else. "When I reach the bridge, Earth will replace the Riders' swamps."

Tamara — or rather, the Baby — was lying either to the Riders or to the humans. She couldn't keep both promises. Didn't the others see that? What made them think the Baby favored them over the Riders?

"Are you saying the Baby will betray the Riders?" Tate asked.

"After they've served their purpose, yes," Tamara said.

"Won't the Riders be mad when you take their habitat away from them?" T.R. asked gently.

"Yes," Tamara said. Tate didn't know if she spoke for herself or the Baby.

"Don't you think they might take it out on us?" T.R. persisted. "If not right away, then eventually. I mean, they're a warrior species. If they decided to eliminate us, we would be slaughtered."

The Baby, peering over Tamara's shoulder, laughed.

"That's true," Tamara said, and a faint smile touched her lips. She turned and walked back to the Riders — row after row of Riders. Eight or ten chiefs came forward to meet her. An impressive force, growing larger by the minute. How had they gathered so quickly?

So much happening so rapidly. Tate could sense Tamara's impatience, the Riders' restlessness. What was the big hurry? Did Tamara know the Blue Meanies were close to taking the bridge?

"Well, I think that went very well," T.R. said.

The others stared.

"We're still alive, are we not?" T.R. asked.

"Yes, but who knows how long that will last," Burroway said darkly. "I keep wondering why the Baby doesn't get rid of us."

"Maybe the Baby is busy with more important things," Tate said. "Maybe we're on its to-do list, just near the bottom." If that was true, she didn't have much time to figure out how to keep them alive.

How do you choose a course when you have no map, no compass, no stars, and no sun to guide you? Jobs turned the problem around in his mind and came up with nothing.

2Face's group of followers had stalled on top of a hill. Mo'Steel and Kubrick were keeping watch. Everyone else was lying down in the grass. Edward had dozed off. Billy was quiet. Asleep or lost in his own thoughts. The rest of them were supposed to be resting, too, but their conversation kept twisting, swirling, turning back on itself.

How to get to the bridge?

"On Earth, we navigate — navigated — by the stars because they were constant," Jobs said. "What's constant in this environment?"

"Change," Violet said petulantly.

Jobs laughed. "True. But that's not much help."

"Squids, Squids, and more Squids," Mo'Steel said.

Jobs looked up. Mo was right. The Squids were growing in number. They were numerous enough to give the sky a strangely beautiful pink color. The automatons behaved much like geese heading south for the winter: They formed flocks and flew in formation. Unlike birds, however, they never had to rest or pause to eat.

"We have to follow the Squids," 2Face said decisively. "They were engineered to protect Mother. They must be heading toward the bridge so they can repair her or reboot her or whatever."

"I agree," Jobs said. "We've got to find the bridge."

"Are you sure now is the right time?" Violet asked. "We're assuming the Blue Meanies and the Squids are heading for a big showdown on the bridge. Are we sure we want to walk into a battle?"

There was a pause while the others considered that.

"We'd be completely vulnerable," Olga said. "We have no weapons, and we saw how easily the Squids killed the Blue Meanie back there."

"We have weapons," Kubrick said. "Our fists."

Noyze laughed. "Your fists might be weapons. Mine aren't."

"I think it would be wiser to wait," Dr. Cohen said.

"No," 2Face said in her usual forceful manner. "We wait and either the Blue Meanies or the Squids will take control of the bridge. The Squids might even manage to get Mother working again. We've got to take control now while the situation is unbalanced."

"Fly low," Mo'Steel said. "Stay under the radar."

"Exactly," 2Face said.

Something was bothering Jobs. Something that didn't quite add up. "Where is Tamara going?" he wondered out loud. "She said she was going to take control of the bridge. But Tamara is heading in the opposite direction as the Squids. Someone is going the wrong way."

"Maybe she had to make a stop first," Noyze suggested.

"A stop for what?" Violet asked.

"Weapons," Kubrick said.

(CHAPTER NINE)

"RIDERS!"

Billy was not asleep. He was aware of the others' conversation. More aware of it than they could ever be.

He heard their words. He sensed feelings that rose, fell, shifted, and mixed like notes in a complicated piece of music. Nine minds harmonizing.

Mo'Steel's excitement. 2Face's smug satisfaction with finally being in charge. Jobs's curiosity. Dr. Cohen's loneliness. 2Face's worry. Kubrick's feelings toward 2Face. 2Face's indifference toward Kubrick. Kubrick's fury with 2Face's indifference. Edward's cozy, sleepy response to seeing his mother's face in a dream.

Some of the emotions came and went faster than Billy could register them. Others — like Olga's affection for her son — never wavered.

Finally Billy closed his mind. He spun the dial and

tried to tune into what else was happening on the ship.

There.

Mother. She was weak, deteriorating fast. Only an echo of what she had been. But still alive. Still dangerous. She was directing thousands of Squids all over the ship, preparing them to go into battle to protect her.

Again Billy spun the dial.

There.

Far away, like fireworks in the next town, the minds of the other Remnants. They were chiming the same high notes over and over. Fear. Indecision. Moral outrage. Anger.

Billy sat up. "Something is happening to the others. They're —" Billy hesitated, unsure of what adjective to choose when so many fit.

Then —

The same panicked high notes. Much clearer, closer. Coming from Mo'Steel and Kubrick.

"Riders!" Mo'Steel shouted. "There has to be thirty of them, coming this way!"

Panic, indecision, fear. The emotions swarming around him made Billy dizzy, nauseous.

"Run!" 2Face ordered.

From the Riders came a chorus of shrieks like the brakes of a runaway train. Their battle cry.

Jobs searching through a field. Unable to find his younger brother because his skin had turned straw-colored and blended into the grass. "Edward! Edward, where are you?"

Edward sitting up with a confused, sleepy expression. Jobs pulling him to his feet, urging him forward.

They were running. Billy with 2Face, Jobs, Edward, Kubrick, and Mo'Steel ahead of him and the others behind. Running in the same direction they'd been heading. Only now the Riders were chasing them.

Down the hill. Slipping, sliding, grass slapping them in the face, unable to see where their feet were landing. Edward fell and rolled until Mo'Steel grabbed him and yanked him up. The bottom of the hill. Water. They splashed through and started up the hill on the other side.

Pointless, futile. They were inchworms trying to outrun greyhounds. The Riders on their hover-boards were closing fast, yelling their bloodthirsty cry.

Billy heard the others' thoughts, jumbled together like a panic variety pack. Horrifying images of death.

The worst were Noyze and Dr. Cohen. They'd never seen Riders and what they imagined was even worse than reality.

Billy couldn't block out the others' minds. Couldn't concentrate on blocking them and run at the same time. They were too persistent, too panicked.

Noyze cried out. Billy shot a look toward the sound. He saw her topple backward, arms flung out, mouth open. She fell and disappeared into the tall grass.

"Someone help!" Dr. Cohen shouted.

Then the Riders were on them, the grass shushing aside to reveal a swarm of hoverboards, each one topped by a warrior with his spear at the ready. The Riders' eating mouths gnashed. They shrieked so loudly that Billy covered his ears. What could they do? They were completely defenseless. The Riders were closing in. Ten feet. Five!

"Get down!" 2Face bellowed.

Billy dropped onto his hands and knees and then onto his belly. His face hit the dirt. He tasted gritty soil on his tongue.

A crash off to his right. The grass waved and Violet rolled into view. They stared at each other, eyes wild, breathing deeply, not daring to speak. Billy was happy it was Violet. Happy that the last thing he would see was her pretty face.

Riders! Two, seven, ten hoverboards rushing at them, blocking out the sky, and then —

They were past!

Past. And Billy was still alive. He blinked. Violet stared, too shocked to move.

Billy stood up. Shaky, dirty, confused. He offered Violet a hand. She got up, brushed the dirt and grass off her dress. Billy turned 360 degrees and saw the heads of his friends appearing in the tall grass around him.

The Riders had already crested the next hill. Their cries were fading into the distance. Violet and Billy began to walk toward 2Face, toward where all of the others were gathering.

Dr. Cohen had a wide, amazed smile. She gave Noyze a sideways hug.

2Face was counting heads like a teacher on a field trip. "Everyone is here," she said briskly.

"You okay?" Olga asked Mo'Steel.

"Fine, Mom. You?" Mo'Steel asked.

"A few scrapes and scratches," Olga said. "Nothing serious."

"Why didn't they wipe us out?" Edward asked.

Jobs shook his head. "Good question."

"They sure seemed to be in a hurry," Violet said.

"Maybe the fight has already started," Jobs said.

"Let's just say we were lucky and leave it at that. We've got to reach the bridge. Time to move." 2Face.

"The others," Billy said. "Tate. Yago. Something is happening to them. Something bad."

Jobs, Violet, and Mo'Steel exchanged looks.

"Can we help them?" Noyze asked.

Billy shrugged. "I — I'm not sure where they are."

One by one, the others turned to 2Face. Waited for her to decide.

"Time to move," she said.

(CHAPTER TEN)

"I GET THE MESSAGE."

The Riders were preparing for battle. Half a dozen chiefs, plus Tamara and the Baby, crouched together in a circle. They drew in the peaty soil with sticks, arguing. Generals planning strategy.

The remaining Riders — the ones Tate thought of as the troops — seemed to be killing time. They fished in the copper-colored sea, built fires, sharpened spears and boomerangs, and drank from small green flasks they carried on their bandoliers.

Tate sat against a tree, eating a piece of fish. One of the Riders had given the little group of humans a crude bowl full of the charred eel-like creatures. The fish was surprisingly delicious, flavored with the smoke from the fire. All Tate could wish for was some salt and pepper. And maybe a plate, a napkin, and a fork and knife.

"Watch out for the bones," Roger Dodger said.

He was nearby, leaning against another one of the endless trees.

T.R. and Burroway were farther off, poking a fire, seemingly lost in their thoughts or regrets. Tate had no desire to join them. Yago was talking quietly and urgently to Anamull and D-Caf. The boys both looked anxious to escape.

"Lots of little bones," Roger Dodger warned her.

"I'll be careful." The others were ignoring Roger Dodger, so Tate had encouraged him to sit with her. He wasn't a bad kid.

"My dad got a trout bone caught in his throat once," Roger Dodger said, starting to giggle. "We were camping. The closest hospital was about fifty miles away and Dad gagged and gagged and finally threw up all over the car."

Tate smiled. "Was he okay?"

"Yeah." Roger Dodger sobered up. "But it doesn't really matter too much now, does it?"

Tate didn't say anything. She wondered what Roger Dodger had been like back on Earth. Probably just a normal kid, playing with his video games and doing homework. Thinking about how much his life had changed made Tate sad.

The Remnants tended to think of themselves as

lucky. After all, they were the ones who had survived. But maybe they'd gotten that backward.

Maybe.

Tate watched as Tamara and the Baby separated from the ever-growing group of Riders and approached T.R. and Burroway's fire. Tamara put the Baby down and helped herself to some of the food. The men moved away silently as Tamara crouched down and began to eat. Exactly the chance Tate had been waiting for.

"I'll be back," Tate told Roger Dodger. She stood up and approached the fire. She picked up a piece of fish and then gave Tamara a tentative smile. "Not bad, huh?"

Tamara's face was like stone. Her eyes showed no warmth, no recognition, no humanity. She could have been a machine.

The Baby reacted by baring its pointy little white teeth at Tate. It crawled between Tamara and Tate and glared in Tate's direction.

"I get the message," Tate said coldly to the Baby. Her stomach was twisting with fear, but she refused to show it. Nobody bullied her. Nobody.

She longed to put a hand on Tamara's shoulder, to let her know she wasn't alone. But that wasn't happening — not with the Baby standing guard.

Reluctantly, Tate retreated to her spot under the trees. Roger Dodger had dozed off, still sitting up.

Tate flashed back on the one moment she'd seen pure humanity shining from Tamara's eyes: when the Baby had transformed into a Shipwright. Then, when the Baby was strong enough to move and speak for itself, the connection with Tamara seemed to have been broken. For those brief moments, Tamara had seemed lost. Tate regretted not approaching her then, not trying to convince her to resist the Baby's control.

So she had missed one opportunity. That didn't mean she could give up. She just had to try again.

But when?

The answer was obvious: when the Baby took another Blue Meanie. It looked as if the Baby was going to have plenty of opportunities, considering the enormous ranks of Riders who were about to declare war on the Meanies.

War.

Tate wasn't thrilled with the idea of turning the Meanies into enemies. The humans' survival seemed precarious enough already. Why antagonize a group of aliens that possessed superior firepower?

She wondered if the Meanies already thought of them as enemies. Mother had forced the humans to attack the Meanies. The battle had been ridiculous — with Yago and his toadies riding in on horseback and the rest of them dressed up like extras in a Civil War regiment. The humans had been completely outgunned. They were lucky the Meanies hadn't turned it into a total massacre.

And then there was Billy.

Billy.

Could it be that the Baby was interested in Billy? Or scared of him?

Tate felt lightning-struck. Maybe she was wrong about the Baby wanting to use Billy or being scared of him. But, even if she was wrong, Billy was the strongest person among them and the most able to help them.

He should know what the Baby was up to.

Tate sat up on her heels, full of energy but unsure of exactly what to do.

First things first. If she was right about the Baby, she had to warn Billy and the others about what was going on. Maybe, if she could find the others quickly, she could be back before the battle began, before the Baby could absorb any more Meanies.

Tate crawled over to Roger Dodger and shook his shoulder. "Wake up," she whispered.

Roger Dodger opened his eyes, silently alert.

"I'm going to go look for the others," Tate told him as quietly as possible. "We need to warn them about Tamara and the Riders."

Roger Dodger bit his lip. "Can I come?"

Tate nodded and got up. "Follow me. Quietly." She turned toward the woods and instantly noticed a figure among the trees — not five feet away.

D-Caf.

And she could tell from his expression that he had heard everything.

CHAPTER ELEVEN

"FASTEN YOUR SEAT BELT!"

Tate stared at D-Caf, listening to her own uneven breathing, waiting for him to call out to Yago and expose their plan. She waved Roger Dodger off. Best to distance him from her betrayal.

"Hey, D-Caf." Roger Dodger took a step back and beamed an innocent smile.

D-Caf glanced over his shoulder. His muscles twitched and his eyes darted as he stepped closer to Tate. Too close. "I want to come with you," he said into her ear, tickling her with his hot breath.

Tate stepped back, looked into D-Caf's jumpy eyes, wondered how long it would take for Yago to notice them talking and demand to know what was going on. "Why?" she asked warily.

"Yago," D-Caf said. "Let's just say I — I could use a break."

Tate blinked. So one of Yago's faithful was doubting him. Interesting. But it could also be a trick. She couldn't trust D-Caf. Couldn't forget he was a killer.

What she needed was a test. A test of his loyalty.

Tate was acutely aware of how tense their little group seemed. "Act casual," she said, taking a few steps away from D-Caf. But, of course, he never acted casual. Wasn't in his repertoire. He swung his upper body from side to side, apparently unable to stand still.

"See those hoverboards?" Tate asked.

D-Caf followed her gaze. Nodded.

Lying against some trees a little ways down the beach were about twenty Rider hoverboards and some weapons. Their owners had wandered down to the water to fish.

Nobody was guarding their gear. Tate didn't know what to make of that. Maybe the Riders were unconcerned because they were among friends and allies. But did they really trust the humans so completely? Maybe this, too, was a trap. It was almost too perfect.

"We'll need two hoverboards and as many weapons as you can carry," Tate told D-Caf. "See if you can get them. Roger Dodger and I will meet you farther into the forest."

D-Caf stared down the beach, considering the risk. Then he nodded. "I'll be right back."

Tate pulled Roger Dodger into the shade of the

trees. They watched as D-Caf moved nervously down the beach. He lingered near the hoverboards for a few minutes. No reaction from the Riders.

Moving quickly and with surprising grace, D-Caf grabbed two of the boards, some weapons, and dragged them into the woods. Still no reaction from the Riders.

"Go!" Tate told Roger Dodger.

They crashed through the forest, quickly intercepting D-Caf. He was rolling the hoverboards like thin wheels, his eyes wide with excitement. "I did it," he said.

"Give me one," Tate said, aware that someone would follow them soon. She laid the hoverboard down among the tree roots and stepped onto it.

The board rose slightly.

Go, Tate thought, and the board instantly responded by zooming toward a nearby tree trunk, steering neatly around it, and heading back to where the boys stood watching. Driving the hoverboard was as easy as moving her legs. The connection was made in a part of her brain she wasn't aware of.

"It works," Roger Dodger said.

"It works," Tate agreed. "I wasn't sure it would. Jobs said these things are linked mentally to their owners."

"Then won't they call them back?" D-Caf asked.

"I'm hoping that if we put enough distance between us and the Riders, the connection will be broken," Tate said. "Come on, Roger Dodger, let's go."

Roger Dodger grabbed a spear and a boomerang. He climbed up onto her board and wrapped his arms around her waist.

D-Caf picked up the second spear and got on the other board. "Which way?"

"Into the trees," Tate said. "We'll have more cover that way. Hopefully we can get far enough away before they even notice the boards are missing."

Then they were riding. Hovering easily over the treacherous roots, skirting tree trunks, ducking to avoid the waving branches. Tate had to push aside her fears to keep up with D-Caf. He was moving fast, maybe too fast, clearly enjoying the ride. She wanted to call to him, tell him to slow down. But she didn't. Speed was the thing. They had to put distance between themselves and the Riders.

What would happen when the Riders noticed the boards were missing and called them back? How suddenly would they lose control? If it happened fast, they'd crash, fall three feet to the ground, hit the tree trunks and gnarled roots, maybe break a bone, maybe shatter a skull. . . .

Two minutes passed.

Then five.

Tate's pulse began to slow. They were doing it. They were getting away.

"These things are great!" Roger Dodger called out.

"Yeah," Tate agreed with a relieved laugh. "You don't even have to stop for gas."

"In fact, if you have gas, it's probably better not to stop!" D-Caf said.

Tate groaned.

Then she heard it.

Loud metallic screams. The Riders' war cry. Tate risked a quick glance back, cursed. Half a dozen Riders! Coming up from behind them and closing fast.

"Let's see what these babies can do!" D-Caf cried, urging his board to go even faster.

Tate did the same. Her board didn't respond. Instead it dipped with a sickening lurch.

"Ahhhh!" Roger Dodger yelled.

Somewhere, maybe back on the beach, the board's owner was trying to call it back.

"Fasten your seat belt!" Tate yelled. "It's going to be a bumpy ride!"

CHAPTER TWELVE

"WRONG WAY, IDIOT!"

Tree! Tree! Tree!

Adrenaline coursed through D-Caf's veins. Fast, faster, still faster. He could feel another voice vying for control of the hoverboard, but it was weak. His own voice was strong.

D-Caf rocketed through the trees, making constant little adjustments to avoid their hundreds of swaying limbs.

Left! Left! Right!

He was a god of hoverboard pilots. The Riders never went this fast. The wimps. They would never catch him. He was uncatchable.

Then, impossibly, a Rider! Moving much too fast, closing in from D-Caf's left side, all of the joints in his legs bent, rust-colored body crouched low, a black tongue extending from his eating head and nervously tasting the air.

Tree! Tree! Tree!

D-Caf couldn't fight at this speed. His only hope was outrunning the Rider. But the Rider was closing in, taking impossible risks, grazing tree trunks, moving diagonally closer and closer to D-Caf, and pulling out his spear with one hand.

D-Caf urged his board on. *Faster, faster, faster.* The tree trunks blurred. The Rider threw his spear. Missed by a mile. Then —

A metallic crunch, the squeal of wood under stress, and a high-pitched wail that clearly translated into "Rider in pain." D-Caf glanced back. The Rider had crashed!

D-Caf slowed down to rubberneck. The Rider's board was shattered into half a dozen jagged pieces.

"Yes!" D-Caf shouted half a second before he felt a jarring impact. D-Caf's teeth slammed down on his tongue. His neck snapped forward, back. He sat down hard. His butt hit thin air and he fell, scraping the back of his calves raw on the edge of the hoverboard. He crashed to the ground, feeling the shock in his tailbone, up his spine. Tasted blood. Rolled over in a fetal position. Breathed in and out. Opened one eye and looked up.

His hoverboard was embedded in a tree trunk.

Pain. In his legs. Racing up and down his spine. Ignore it. Ignore it and get up before the Riders turned his head into an hors d'oeuvre.

D-Caf cursed, pulled himself onto his knees, then slowly stood up. He retrieved his spear and boomerang from among the roots and stood waiting for whatever would come through the woods.

Tate.

Thank god it was Tate!

Her hoverboard was jerking like a bucking bronco. Roger Dodger was down on his knees, reaching his arms way out to hold onto the edges of the board. The main group of Riders was a hundred feet behind them.

Boomerang!

It hit a tree branch, veered off to the left, shot back toward the Riders.

Boomerang!

Heading straight toward D-Caf's eyes. He ducked, rolled, stood up woozily. That was close. Too close.

"Tate!" D-Caf called. "Pick me up!"

Tate approached with agonizing slowness. Her board lurched forward, lurched back. D-Caf ran to meet it, took Tate's outstretched hand, pulled himself up onto the board. The board sank down six inches, then steadied.

"Too much weight," Tate said.

"It's holding for now," D-Caf said. It was crowded on the board, but not too crowded. "Let go of it! Let me drive!"

"I can drive!" Tate inched over to make room for him. "You're the one who crashed."

"You drive like my grandmother," D-Caf said. "Let me drive or we're going to die."

"Let him drive!" Roger Dodger yelled.

"Fine, perfect," Tate mumbled. "Just watch the trees."

D-Caf felt Tate relinquish control over the board.

Go, he thought. The board responded by jerking forward a foot. Another voice was here, calling the board back.

Sorry, D-Caf thought. *That ain't happening.*

The Riders were circling. Moving to the left and right. Cutting off their escape. A spear passed inches in front of D-Caf's nose. He hadn't even seen it coming. His stomach felt cold with fear.

Desperate, D-Caf fought the other voice for control of the board. They picked up a little speed.

Then a little more. But they were still moving so slowly. Pitifully slowly.

"Rider!" Roger Dodger yelled. "Right behind us!"

D-Caf didn't look. Didn't dare take his eyes off the trees ahead.

"Duck! Now, now, now!" Tate yelled. "Do it!"

D-Caf ducked, felt a breath of air as a boomerang grazed his scalp, close enough to trim his hair. "Man, I hate those things," he mumbled, easing back into a stand.

"Still coming!" Tate warned.

D-Caf saw a sudden movement as Tate brought up one of the spears. Then — the *clang, clang, clang* of metal on metal. Tate grunting with effort. Unless she was hiding a past as an Olympic fencing champion, Tate would be shish kebab any second.

"Faster!" Roger Dodger yelled.

"Get the boomerang!" Tate yelled.

D-Caf tried some evasive maneuvers to shake off the Rider. Jerked the board left. Left again. Now right.

Clang, clang!

"What do I do with the boomerang?!" Roger Dodger sounded as if he were coming unhinged.

"Aim it and throw!" Tate said.

"I don't know how!"

"Pretend it's a Frisbee."

The board was picking up speed. D-Caf focused on steering through the trees. Faster, faster. He had to get through before the Riders completely surrounded them.

"Great shot!" Tate yelled.

Roger Dodger laughed. "Yeah!"

"Is he hurt?" D-Caf demanded, eyes still trained on the trees. "If he's hurt or dead, we've got to get his board."

"Not hurt *or* dead," Tate said. "Still coming."

"There's another one on our right!" Roger Dodger announced.

"Watch it, the boomerang is coming back!" Tate said.

"I'll catch it," Roger Dodger said.

"Do you *like* having fingers?" Tate said. "Let it go! Coming on our right. Move left, move, move!"

D-Caf couldn't move. He had to watch the trees, had to keep the board balanced. He steered left, swerved to avoid crashing, felt a burn, the boomerang slicing through the flesh of his thigh, a disturbing wetness, an electric pain.

"Ahhh!"

D-Caf's concentration faltered. The board dropped, spun 180 degrees, headed back toward the bleeding Rider who was still pursuing them. The other voice had gained control of the board. More Riders were closing in from the sides. Six of them. Maybe more. Hard to count.

"Wrong way, idiot!" Roger Dodger yelled.

Tate let loose with a vibrant string of curse words.

D-Caf ignored them both. Tried to block out the pain in his leg. Managed to fight the other voice until the board's forward movement halted and they were just hanging in the air, suspended above the ground.

Riders crowded in on three sides. One swung his spear at Tate, missed, pitched forward awkwardly.

"They're totally out of it!" D-Caf yelled.

Tate shot him a quick, puzzled look.

D-Caf tried to convince the board to get moving. Nothing doing. He picked up a spear, jabbed at the Rider on his right, missed, dodged the Rider's clumsy blow, cursed at the board, jabbed again and again, felt his spear hit home and the board lurch backward.

Tate and Roger Dodger and the Riders were yelling, punching, kicking. D-Caf's Rider was down on his knees. His board slowly sank to the ground.

D-Caf yanked his spear out, ignored the purple blood, jumped to the ground, sending a blinding pain through his leg.

He mounted the fallen Rider's board, rose up, swooped around, and nailed Roger Dodger's Rider with a boomerang. Roger Dodger jumped onto the now-empty board.

The Riders backed off, turned, vanished through the trees. Tate, D-Caf, and Roger Dodger hovered, each on their own board, breathing heavily, staring at one another in disbelief.

"We scared them off!" Roger Dodger said.

Tate shook her head wearily. "I think Tamara called them back. Could mean the battle is starting."

"My thigh," D-Caf said. "It's cut pretty bad."

Tate made them land while she bandaged D-Caf's thigh with scraps of their clothing. Blood oozed through the bandages almost immediately. D-Caf felt light-headed from pain.

Two dead Riders lay on the roots. Roger Dodger picked up their bandoliers and weapons. The bandoliers didn't fit Roger Dodger, but Tate and D-Caf each strapped one on. Roger Dodger kept a spear.

They rode down to the beach and began skimming along, staying near the trees, searching for

2Face's group. The sun was setting, a breeze kicking up from the water.

D-Caf's leg began to throb. His brain picked up the rhythm. *Pain, pain, pain, pain, pain. At least I'm not dead,* he thought. D-Caf smiled to himself. Smiled with pride. He'd faced the Riders without bunnying out. He was a warrior. And a fantastic hoverboard pilot.

Strange sensation, pride.

Nice.

(CHAPTER THIRTEEN)

"IT'S SUICIDE."

Fléchette guns.

Jobs and the others had been hearing them for some time now. They were getting louder. Jobs thought he could recognize other sounds, too: Blue Meanies' rocket packs firing, the low explosions of the Squids' jet weapons, irregular thuds. Other sounds of human battle — shouts, moans, cries — were missing. That wasn't surprising considering that the Blue Meanies communicated with sign language and the Squids were silent.

Jobs trudged along behind Mo'Steel. He felt subdued, anxious. Arguing about walking into a battle was one thing. Actually doing it was another.

Nobody was talking much. Olga and Dr. Cohen were a bit breathless from climbing a hill. Back on Earth, the hill wouldn't have been considered very high. But here in the Rider environment, it was practically a mountain.

The sky was thick with Squids, more Squids than Jobs imagined existed. They seemed to be converging somewhere just up ahead.

Kubrick, Mo'Steel, and 2Face reached the top of the hill first. They stood motionless, not speaking. When Jobs joined them, he could see why.

In the valley below, a full-scale battle was under way. The scene was vast, complex, confusing — like watching, from above, the final fight scene in a big-budget Hollywood movie.

"No sign of Tamara, Yago, and the others," 2Face said.

No. The extras in this battle scene were Squids and Blue Meanies. Neither group of aliens seemed interested in the humans' presence. They were nothing more than observers, trying to make sense of the scene unfolding below them.

The Squids were converging onto the battle from all directions, many passing directly over the Remnants' heads, others coming in over the copper-colored sea that stretched out on the left side of the battle. The valley was thick with Blue Meanies — some on the ground, some flying at low altitude, and all of them firing fléchette guns at the approaching Squids and killing them in large numbers.

Jobs focused on one Meanie, followed the burst from his gun, watched it bring down one Squid after another. The Squids fell to the ground, littering the grassy valley. They were dying by the thousands, but more and more kept coming. A seemingly endless supply.

The Squids were fairly helpless in the air. Some were shooting matter bursts at the Meanies — but air is not very massive and the bursts were weak. The Squids that made it through the fléchette gun-fire and landed were shooting much more powerful bursts. The Blue Meanies they hit were going down fast.

Most of the Squids that made it through were landing on the ground just in front of a structure that certainly wasn't part of the Rider environment. Jobs figured it was part of the ship.

The structure was a stack of perfectly square metal platforms placed one on top of another. The top platform was about the size of Jobs's bedroom at home. It was filled with three rows of platforms of diminishing size, each containing three chairs and sitting on a shallow raised disk. The chair platforms were surrounded by a railing with a narrow opening to walk through. This structure had the patina of age. The metal was mottled, pitted, and worn.

"It looks like a pyramid," 2Face said.

"Yes," Violet agreed. "But I doubt it's a tomb or a temple. It's very plain. Almost austere."

"It's some sort of transportation system, has to be," Jobs said. "Probably no more important or noteworthy to the Shipwrights than a toaster or a car was important to us humans back on Earth."

"Transportation to where?" Kubrick asked.

"The bridge," Jobs said.

"What makes you think that?" 2Face asked. "Wishful thinking?"

"No, the battle," Jobs said. "Why would the Meanies and Squids be fighting over this structure if it wasn't important?"

"How do you think it works?" Olga asked wearily.

Jobs pointed to the only decoration on the structure — a sort of frieze or mural made up of pure geometric shapes that ran along the lower level of the pyramid.

"I think those may be the controls," Jobs said.

"Billy, do you think you could interface with it?" Mo'Steel asked. "Like you did with Mother?"

"I could try," Billy said.

"Just one problem," Violet said. "The Squids are obviously trying to stop the Meanies from accessing the structure. What makes you think we'll be able to get through?"

"I think it's possible Mother didn't program the Squids to attack humans," Jobs said. "We just may be able to stroll in without the Squids paying any attention."

"What about the Blue Meanies?" 2Face asked. "Mother doesn't program them."

"I'm hoping the Squids will keep them busy," Jobs said.

"How comforting," 2Face said wryly.

"Let's try it," Mo'Steel said.

"You kids are crazy," Olga argued. "You're suggesting we just waltz into the middle of that battle? It's suicide. Even if the Squids and the Meanies aren't firing at us, chances are we'll get hit with a stray bullet or worse."

Mo'Steel pointed off to the left. "We go that way, Mom. Down the hill, take a quick, refreshing swim, and come up behind the line of battle."

"I'll go first," Kubrick said. "See if I draw any fire."

"Good idea," 2Face agreed. "Jobs, Billy — you two go next. Get to the controls as quickly as you can and try to figure out how that thing works. The rest of us will follow. Mo, I want you with me, bringing up the rear."

Mo'Steel's shoulders drooped and the excitement faded out of his face. He nodded reluctantly.

Violet put a hand on Edward's shoulder and gave Jobs a weak smile. Jobs smiled back, grateful that Violet was offering to keep an eye on his little brother.

"See you on the bridge." Kubrick gave them a loose salute, turned, and began trotting down the hill toward the shore.

Jobs and Billy waited until Kubrick was halfway down the hill. He didn't attract any fire so they started after him. Jobs matched Billy's pace, which was slightly slower than his own. Down the grassy slope. Eyes on Kubrick's back, the exposed muscles of his neck and skull. Down, trying to forget about the battle waging below them. Down, trying not to worry about Edward and the others.

Think about what's important, Jobs told himself. *The controls.*

He itched to examine them. And now, because of that desire, half of what was left of the human race was marching into serious danger. He wasn't even sure he could figure out the controls. Alien technology. Designed to do — he didn't know what exactly.

Maybe this whole idea wasn't too smart.

"Kubrick!" Billy yelled.

Jobs jerked to attention in time to see a matter blast nail Kubrick. Kubrick hit the ground and began to roll downhill. His body was smoking.

"Is he dead?" Jobs demanded. Kubrick's skin didn't feel pain, but that didn't mean he could withstand a blast like that.

"Not dead," Billy said.

Jobs looked up. Squid. Just one. Directly overhead. Another second and it would fire on them. "Split up!" Jobs yelled. "Run!"

CHAPTER FOURTEEN

"IMPROVISE."

Mo'Steel saw the Squid hit Kubrick. He saw Jobs and Billy fleeing for their lives. His heart lifted. So much for bringing up the rear. Time for some action.

He had to stop that Squid.

But how?

The automaton was twenty feet above him in the air. Mo'Steel had no weapon. His only hope was to somehow lure the Squid down to the ground.

But how?

Improvise, Mo'Steel told himself.

"Everyone — get down!" 2Face yelled. "Don't make yourself an easy target!"

Would that work? Wouldn't the Squids have a more sophisticated way of locating targets? Heat sensors? Infrared vision? Mo'Steel would have to ask Jobs. If either of them lived that long.

As the others hit the ground, Mo'Steel ran forward. "Yo — Mr. Squid!" he yelled. "You think you're all that? Let's see if you can hit me!"

Ignoring Mo'Steel, the Squid fired at Billy. Missed. Jobs was following Kubrick's lead. He was rolling down the hill, half hidden by the grasses.

"Stay down!" Mo'Steel yelled at Billy.

Billy dropped to his knees, out of Mo'Steel's sight.

"Hey, calamari face! Over here!" Mo'Steel yelled.

Now, for whatever reason, the Squid was paying attention. It turned to Mo'Steel, tentacles waving. Fired! Mo'Steel dodged. A small patch of grass went up in flames.

Mo'Steel felt more confident. The blasts weren't that powerful. Even if he got hit, he'd live. Probably.

"Missed me, missed me, now you've got to kiss me!" Mo'Steel taunted. He ran in a zigzag pattern toward the water.

The Squid fired three times.

Missed. Missed. Missed.

The Squid closed in, flying lower and lower, and aiming with more and more accuracy. Mo'Steel felt the heat of several near misses.

The Squid landed four feet in front of Mo'Steel. Fired.

Mo'Steel dove to his left, somersaulted, came up on his feet. Now that the Squid was on the ground, the heat of the blast was ten times more powerful.

Only one safe place to be, Mo'Steel thought. He ran straight at the Squid and landed on its back. He was facing the Squid's head with its tentacles behind him. Mo'Steel grabbed on with his knees, sank his fingertips into rubbery pink Squid skin.

The Squid went wild. It jumped three feet into the air, twisting, turning, trying to knock Mo'Steel free. Mo'Steel could feel an odd vibration rumbling through the automaton. A dozen tentacles lashed at Mo'Steel, hitting him in the face, back, arms, legs. Wherever sucker pads hit bare skin, Mo'Steel felt like a jellyfish was stinging him. Highly unpleasant. But not intolerable.

And the view was pretty good. Mo'Steel could see Billy wading awkwardly though the copper-colored sea. Jobs had already emerged. He was running toward the pyramid, intent on the controls.

The Squid spun 180 degrees, tossed its backside high into the air, rose another eight feet in the air. Mo'Steel rode the momentum forward and back, his butt coming up off the Squid's back, his knees firmly anchored.

With astounding speed, the Squid changed directions — twisting the opposite way. Mo'Steel slid sideways but quickly righted himself. One of the tentacles wrapped around his neck. Mo'Steel had to remove one hand to yank the tentacle off. The Squid jerked left, right, left — trying to unseat him. Mo'Steel held on.

Again, the weird rumbling moved through the Squid.

The others were in the water now. Mo'Steel could see his mother looking anxiously up at him. Jobs and Billy were at the controls, frantically running their hands over the frieze of circles, squares, and triangles.

Another Squid! Flying toward them.

Mo'Steel crouched low over his Squid's back, figuring he was safe as long as he stayed close. The new Squid couldn't hit him without taking out its buddy.

Again, weird vibrations passed through his Squid. Was it communicating with the other one? Maybe at a frequency too high for humans to hear? It made sense that the automatons would have some way to communicate, to coordinate their efforts.

Automatons.

It hit Mo'Steel about half a second before the new Squid fired. Squids weren't human. They were machines designed to get a job done. They didn't value life.

No time to react. No time to plan.

Uh-oh, Mo'Steel thought.

The matter blast hit Mo'Steel's Squid directly between the eyes. The Squid went limp, began to plunge toward the ground. Mo'Steel lost his grip. Cartwheeled through the air. Hit something hard. The ground? No, not the ground. A tentacle! Hit again and this time hung on.

The fried Squid hit the water. Mo'Steel landed on top of it and sank, the air knocked out of him, his fall broken by the Squid's rubbery flesh.

Mo'Steel fell through the coppery water. He stayed under, stayed under, stayed under. He wanted the attacking Squid to think he was dead. Otherwise, he actually would be. Finally, lungs burning, he surfaced. He checked the sky, found it empty, took a deep, shaky breath, and broke out into a grin.

What a woolly ride! What a rush! Had any of the others seen? He spun around, trying to get his bearings.

Mo'Steel heard shouts — coming from the hill

above him. He was confused. Weren't the others on the pyramid? Still dizzy, Mo'Steel looked uphill and was surprised to see Tate, D-Caf, and Roger Dodger skimming toward him on hoverboards.

"Hey!" he called. "Nice boards!"

CHAPTER FIFTEEN

"THIS SMELLS LIKE TROUBLE."

So much was happening all at once — the Blue Meanies massacring the Squids, Billy and Jobs hacking into the controls, Mo'Steel falling from the sky. 2Face didn't know where to turn her attention.

Edward tugged on her sleeve. "Look!"

2Face turned in time to see Tate, Roger Dodger, and D-Caf skimming to Mo'Steel's rescue on Rider hoverboards.

"What are they doing back here?" 2Face wondered out loud.

Noyze and Violet turned to stare.

"Where did they get those hoverboards?" Noyze asked.

"This smells like trouble," 2Face said.

They watched as Tate held out a hand and pulled Mo'Steel out of the water. The foursome started toward the beach on the hoverboards, Mo'Steel riding with Tate. Dr. Cohen and Olga were already running down to the beach to meet them.

2Face looked at Jobs. "You and Billy, stay here. Keep working."

Jobs nodded distractedly. He and Billy had managed to get the control panel powered up. The shapes on the frieze glowed with a strange phosphorescent light. Yellow, green, orange. But now Billy and Jobs seemed at a loss as they urgently discussed what to do next.

2Face headed down to the beach. Kubrick trudged silently along beside her. He seemed to have elected himself 2Face's personal bodyguard. The way he was always hanging around ground on her nerves. She could take care of herself.

Tate and the others rode their boards up onto the beach and landed them. Olga and Dr. Cohen began shooting questions at them. The answers came back jumbled.

"Romeo, you okay?"

"Where did you get those hoverboards?"

"Actually, I could go for some calamine lotion. That Squid stung me."

"Where are the others?"

"What happened to your leg, D-Caf?"

"They're okay. They're still with Tamara."

Tate's gaze was locked on 2Face. "I have news."

"What's up?" 2Face asked.

"Nothing good," Tate said. "Tamara is rounding up the Riders. Any minute now an army of them will come over that hill and attack the Blue Meanies and the Squids. We need to figure out how to stay alive when that happens."

2Face narrowed her eyes, considering.

Could she trust Tate? 2Face hadn't forgotten Tate was the only one who'd tried to save her when Yago decided to feed her to the Baby.

But Tate was always sucking up to Tamara. And she'd chosen to follow Tamara, not 2Face. Could this be a trick? 2Face couldn't imagine how Tate had gotten the hoverboards without Tamara's help. But what would Tamara gain by having them think she was about to ride into battle?

Tate was watching her closely. "Where's Billy?" she asked finally. "I think he should know about this."

2Face felt her temper flare. She was in charge here! Not Billy. Who did Tate think she was to make demands?

Billy laid his right hand gently on a glowing yellow triangle and called out to Mother.

Nothing.

Billy had connected with Mother before. The intensity of the experience had been overwhelming and deeply frightening, and yet Billy longed to relive it. He felt Mother understood him in a way none of the Remnants ever could. In a way no human ever could.

Nothing! Billy felt overcome by sadness when he realized all he could hear in his mind were humans' minds. Jobs's was the loudest and most persistent, circling around and around the same problem: How could they control the pyramid? Neurons fired and synapses snapped as Jobs's frantic mind offered up idea after idea and shot them down again and again.

Billy was getting a headache. Then he felt a sudden nervous thrill pass through Noyze. Blue Meanies — coming this way!

"Blue Meanies — coming this way!" Noyze yelled.

Billy looked toward the valley. Several dozen of the aliens were flying in a low formation directly toward them. Their legs hung loose in the air, tentacles waving slowly.

"We've got to go!" Violet said.

"Go!" Jobs yelled. He paused to pull on Billy's arm. "Come on, buddy! The Meanies are onto us."

Billy hesitated. Where was Mother? Why

couldn't he reach her? He felt an overwhelming loneliness.

Violet, Edward, and Noyze were running. Off the pyramid, onto the beach. 2Face, Tate, D-Caf, and Roger Dodger were already streaking down the peat-moss-like sand. Mo'Steel was hanging back, urging on Olga and Dr. Cohen.

Jobs yanked harder on Billy's arm. "Give it up!" he yelled. "We've got to go!"

Jobs's fear shrilled painfully in Billy's head.

Billy couldn't take it anymore. He had to calm Jobs down, had to quiet the noise in his head. He turned away from the pyramid and ran.

Running itself was pointless. Anyone could see that. Another few seconds and the Meanies would destroy the humans.

Billy would die.

He would never speak to Mother again.

He hoped she wouldn't be lonely after he was gone.

CHAPTER SIXTEEN

"THIS IS GOING TO GET UGLY."

The Blue Meanies fired. Fléchettes! The ground just in front of Jobs and Billy exploded, chunks of soil flying. Run or take cover? Run!

Billy seemed distracted or dazed. Jobs grabbed his hand and pulled him as fast as possible. He braced for the next volley of fléchettes.

He made it five feet. Ten. Fifteen.

Still the Blue Meanies didn't fire.

Then Jobs noticed Olga, Mo'Steel, 2Face, and the others in front of him. They weren't running. They were frozen rigid, mouths open, eyes wide, staring back into the valley with disbelief.

Jobs spun around.

Riders — thousands of Riders! — were spilling over the surrounding hills. They rode hoverboard to hoverboard in row after row. Each had his spear at the ready.

At the very front was Tamara. She had a Rider bandolier slung across her chest and the Baby strapped to her back. Jobs could see the Baby's gleaming white teeth. It was laughing.

The Blue Meanies who had been attacking them turned back. They had bigger problems than a few humans.

"Over here! Over here!" Noyze was shouting.

Yago, Anamull, T.R., and Burroway were running slowly down the beach. They were on foot and they looked ragged, exhausted, and terrified. T.R. managed a weary wave of acknowledgment and they headed toward the other Remnants. Jobs was relieved to see them alive.

Back on the battlefield, Tamara shook a spear over her head. The Riders responded by letting loose a shrieking war cry that echoed through the valley and came close to making Jobs pee in his pants.

He had a strange feeling the Blue Meanies felt the same way. They were swirling in the air almost like a flock of frightened birds. They seemed confused. Did they have a way of communicating over distances?

"Take cover!" Tate shouted. "This is going to get ugly."

Cover, Jobs thought. That was a good idea. But

where? They were surrounded by beach and ocean. The woods were far behind them and apparently filled with Riders.

"Around the side of the pyramid!" 2Face shouted. "Maybe they won't notice us there."

2Face began to run. Jobs and the others followed, with Yago and his group lagging behind, obviously exhausted. They climbed two of the metal platforms and then inched closer to the front of the pyramid. Jobs crouched down with Edward, Mo'Steel, Billy, and Violet nearby and looked back toward the battlefield.

The Blue Meanies were in trouble. Serious trouble.

The sky was dark with hundreds, thousands of Rider boomerangs. They were shredding the Meanies as they flew around in confusion.

Scores of injured or stunned or dead Meanies fell to the ground.

Occasionally Jobs could see the Baby's head emerge from above the chaos.

"The Meanies are getting slaughtered," Mo'Steel said.

"Better than them slaughtering us," 2Face said.

"Except this is what the Baby wants," Tate said

tensely. "It can use a dozen dead Meanies and become a Shipwright. Permanently."

"Then what?" Jobs asked.

Tate shrugged. "Then it does whatever it wants to do, I guess."

"Maybe we ought to sneak away," 2Face said. "Find the bridge before this battle ends."

"No," Burroway said. "Tamara told us to be quiet and stay out of the way and that's what we're going to do."

"In case you forgot, not all of us are following Tamara —" 2Face said angrily.

She was interrupted by an eerie, intense sound. Jobs didn't hear it so much as feel it in his chest and molars. The sound made Jobs want to whimper.

"Where's it coming from?" Violet asked.

Jobs scanned the battlefield, the sky, and then pointed at an airborne Meanie whose tentacles were stuck straight out in a very unnatural way. Violet and Jobs followed the Meanie's line of fire.

The Meanie was aiming at a Rider. One second, the Rider was racing around his peers, triumphantly holding a Meanie head high, and preparing for a little snack. The next second, the Rider's hoverboard flew straight up and he landed on his rear.

"Ha!" Mo'Steel yelled. "The Meanies have an ejector button!"

"Cool!" Edward yelled. "And look — they're sprouting wings!"

One in ten Meanies were growing or deploying wings big enough to support a small airplane. The gleaming, silvery, deadly looking things sprang out of the arched part of their suits like twin ten-foot switchblades. Jobs couldn't stop looking at them. They transformed the Blue Meanies from something merely scary into something terrifying.

"I've never seen those," Dr. Cohen breathed. "Never once in all the hours we watched the Blue Meanies train and take target practice."

"A secret weapon," 2Face said.

"What makes you think they're a weapon?" Noyze demanded.

As if on that signal, one of the Meanies buzzed low over the ranks of Riders and cut them down like a harvester moving through a row of corn. A bewildered hush. Then —

Mayhem.

Riders retreating. Gliding away from the swooping Blue Meanies, trying to reach the safety of the trees. Other Riders holding their ground. Throwing spears and boomerangs into the air, trying to bring down the winged Meanies. Tamara in the middle of it all. Arms in the air. Mouth open as she shouted orders none of the Riders seemed to be obeying.

The Baby wasn't smiling now.

CHAPTER SEVENTEEN

"WE ARE NO LONGER SLAVES."

Sergeant Tamara Hoyle felt weak, ill, desperate. The Baby was furious. So furious that Tamara wanted nothing more than to put things right.

But how?

Tamara didn't know. The Baby wasn't sending her any information. She had no way of reaching out, of asking the Baby what she could do to help. Their communication went only one way.

Tamara wasn't sure how much time had passed since she'd woken on the shuttle. However long it had been, the Baby had been there, inside her brain.

The connection was gentle at first. But its power grew quickly until there was very little of Tamara remaining, until she felt she had no purpose other than following the Baby's orders.

The Baby hadn't bothered with minutiae. It

hadn't told her when to eat or stopped her from chatting aimlessly with Tate. But it had controlled all of the important things, had provided Tamara with a purpose, had spared her the difficulty of figuring things out on her own.

But now, increasingly, the Baby seemed distracted.

All Tamara could feel was rage. She stood in the middle of the battlefield, surrounded by injured and dead Blue Meanies, Squids, and Riders. Blue Meanies were cutting the Riders down by the dozens. Tamara could no longer tell who was winning.

She watched a winged Meanie fly in at a low altitude, heading directly for the Baby. Instinctively Tamara stepped between the Baby and the Meanie. The Meanie wore the suit of a warrior — a golden symbol on its head marking it. The other Meanies were falling back, making room for their military leader. It awkwardly folded its two ten-foot wings and landed near Tamara. An emissary or a threat?

Tamara felt the grasp of the Baby's mind and a wave of relief and pleasure flowed through her.

The Baby sent Tamara the Meanie's name: Most Radiant Sun.

The name was followed by words the Baby wished Tamara to speak. "You have learned a few tricks," she said to the Meanie. "Those are not the same power suits we built for you."

Most Radiant Sun lowered and raised its head slowly, acknowledging the Baby's compliment. This was something Tamara had not known before. The Meanies, or at least some of the Meanies, understood human speech. She watched as the warrior leaned back to expose the panel on its chest. Words scrolled slowly across it.

"The Children have evolved," they read. "We are no longer slaves of the Shipwrights."

"That is why you must perish." Tamara felt her mouth forming the words. Then she felt an immense power flow through her. She knew what she had to do. She had to destroy Most Radiant Sun. It was a fully armed Meanie. She had no weapons. But the Baby would help her.

With the Baby's help, she would prevail.

Tamara felt her vision shift. The warrior still stood in front of her. But now she could see into its suit. She could see inside its hairless wrinkled skin to nerves and tendons and blood coursing along a rather primitive system of veins and arteries. She could see chemicals moving in its mind and knew they were calculating its odds of survival.

Blood surged through Tamara's muscles. Her

nerves tingled. She focused her attention within the Meanie, grasping for its core.

It would use fléchettes first.

Then its two mini-missiles.

For some reason, it wasn't anxious to fight Tamara with its cutting wings.

Most Radiant Sun raised its front leg and let loose a stream of fléchette fire. Tamara jumped impossibly high, flipped in the air, came down, and grabbed an abandoned hoverboard. Her movements were a blur of speed.

The Meanie adjusted its aim. Tamara used the hoverboard like a shield. The Meanie fired until the hoverboard was laced with holes.

Tamara tossed it aside. She ran at top speed through the littered battlefield, dodging fléchettes.

There were abandoned weapons everywhere. Tamara swooped down, snatched them up — spear! boomerang! boomerang! — and tossed them blindly over her shoulder.

Most Radiant Sun veered left, right, left, avoiding the barrage. It kept firing. Tamara heard a whizzing noise as the fléchettes passed inches from her ear.

Then — a pause. Most Radiant Sun was out of fléchettes.

A squeal like a massive bottle rocket. The first

mini-missile! It hit just to Tamara's left. Soil rained down on her hair, her face. She did a back flip, soaring high in the air, landing out of harm's way.

Another squeal. Tamara looked up and saw the mini-missile falling directly toward her. She reached up and caught it barehanded. Then, spinning 180 degrees, she tossed it back into the Meanie's face.

Most Radiant Sun backpedaled. Too late! The missile kaboomed inches from its face, tearing one of its front legs from its body. Most Radiant Sun stumbled forward.

Tamara grabbed a spear and ran toward the Meanie. But Most Radiant Sun had fired its rockets. Before Tamara could reach it, it was airborne, circling around the battlefield in a big arc.

Now the big cutting wings were coming out. Slowly. Ponderously. Most Radiant Sun was still struggling to get the unfolding under control as it swooped toward Tamara.

She ducked easily. Ducked and at the same time thrust the spear upward toward the Meanie. It was too high.

As it turned away from her, Tamara saw the vulnerability. With the big wings deployed, the Meanie couldn't see what was happening behind it. It had a blind spot the size of a Greyhound bus.

Tamara ran, easily catching up with the Meanie. She drew the spear back and threw it like a javelin. The spear flew through the air and hit home in the back of the Meanie's neck, quivering there.

The Meanie lost altitude fast. It crashed headfirst into the ground.

Tamara turned and walked back to the Baby, proud, her duty done. She was surprised to see the Baby wasn't laughing or clapping. Its eyes were hooded with exhaustion, its skin bright with sweat, its shoulders stooped forward. Tamara felt the superhuman energy flow out of her. She stumbled, almost too weary to hold herself upright.

(CHAPTER EIGHTEEN)

"MORE! I WANT MORE."

The Baby wanted power.

Tamara, in spite of her exhaustion, knew what she had to do. She hoisted the Baby onto one hip and staggered toward Most Radiant Sun. She kicked aside its broken wings and tore open its dinged and battered suit.

As soon as the Blue Meanie's skinny legs and rubbery-looking skin were exposed, the Baby shifted eagerly and held his pudgy arms out. Tamara lowered the Baby toward Most Radiant Sun. The Baby touched the rubbery skin. The Blue Meanie's body instantly dissolved and the Baby began to glow.

Tamara could feel the glow, the warmth, as the Baby's brown skin flushed red.

The Baby began to expand, to become a crea-ture humanoid in shape but with short, stubby arms that ended in four tapered fingers. Its legs were long and had extra knees. A triangular protrusion resembling a starfish's arm grew straight from the creature's shoulders. This one protrusion was opaque. The rest of the creature's body was transparent and its organs were clearly visible.

As the Baby transformed into a Shipwright, a shock went through the battlefield. Hoverboards swerved out of control and Meanies stopped firing their weapons as they realized a Shipwright was in their midst. The Riders recovered first and attacked with renewed vigor. Many of the Meanies swooped silently away toward the hills. They seemed unnerved, and the Riders quickly began to dominate the battle.

"More!" the Baby said inside Tamara's head. Before she could move to obey, the strange creature turned its featureless head toward a Blue Meanie that lay injured on the battlefield. As if spellbound, the Meanie rose and approached the Shipwright.

Now the Shipwright grew even larger, towering at least two feet above Tamara. She could no longer recognize any of herself in the creature, no longer trick herself into believing this creature was somehow her offspring.

The Baby was gone. And so was Tamara's connection to it. She felt empty, turned off, dead. All she could do was watch the Shipwright and pray the connection would return.

The Shipwright looked toward the sky.

Tamara mimicked the movement.

A flying wedge of Blue Meanies was bearing down on the Shipwright. The Shipwright yelled to the Riders in their language, and they moved back.

"Get away!" came the Baby's voice in Tamara's head.

She ran, stumbling over the battlefield debris, following the Riders.

The Blue Meanies opened fire, blasting the loose ground around the Shipwright with a solid wall of mini-missiles and fléchettes, enough firepower to shred an entire platoon of Marines. The ground shook, hurling Tamara to her knees.

The Shipwright was a blur of movement.

When the Meanies' barrage finally stopped, the Shipwright stood in the exact position it had held at the beginning. The Riders surrounding Tamara broke into their screeching war cry. The Shipwright turned toward them and bowed its milky white head. Then it strode toward the platform on its long, thin legs.

"Watch out!" Tamara yelled.

A Blue Meanie on the ground raised its firing leg

and pointed its fléchette gun at the Shipwright. The Shipwright barely broke stride as it turned casually, held up one hand. The Meanie imploded, giving off a small puff of blue-black smoke.

The Riders began fanning out across the battlefield, taking out the few Meanies too weak or stubborn to run away.

The Shipwright reached the pyramid. It rhythmically tapped its long fingers over a series of circles, squares, rectangles. The lowest level of the pyramid began to glow with a beautiful silvery light. The light moved up level by level until the entire pyramid was lit. The Shipwright began to climb the side of the pyramid.

Tamara rushed after the Shipwright. She scrambled up the levels of the pyramid, her exhausted thighs burning with the effort. By the time the Shipwright reached the highest level, she was only a few steps behind.

The Shipwright moved through the railing and stepped onto the closest raised circular platform. The platform took on a dim glow.

Tamara couldn't let the Shipwright out of her sight. Without the Shipwright, she was a soldier without a general. Aimless. She dashed forward, stepping onto the platform next to the Shipwright, not caring if she died for her brashness. The Shipwright turned slightly toward her.

Tamara expected the Shipwright to be angry. She prepared herself. The platform became a giant pillar and carried Tamara and the Shipwright into the sky.

CHAPTER NINETEEN

"MOM, I LIVE FOR DANGEROUS."

The Shipwright passed a few feet in front of Mo'Steel. Tamara wasn't far behind. Mo'Steel watched as the pyramid began to glow with light. It didn't take a computer genius to know the Shipwright had somehow activated it.

"If we want to find the bridge, now is the time to hitch a ride," Mo'Steel said.

"Let's go," Billy said.

"I'm in," Jobs said, his brown eyes troubled.

Behind Jobs, Mo'Steel's mother was shaking her head. "Romeo, I don't want you to do it. We don't know anything about this — this machine. It could be beyond dangerous."

"Mom, I live for dangerous." Mo'Steel would have liked to give his mother more time to argue, not that he would have listened, but he had to hurry. "Follow me!" he said.

Mo'Steel grabbed Billy's arm and pulled him to his feet. They climbed the metal platforms of the pyramid as quickly as possible and arrived just in time to see Tamara and the Shipwright disappear from view.

"This one." Billy stepped onto the middle platform on the first row.

Mo'Steel jumped on next to him. "Hey — where's Jobs?"

"He's coming," Billy said.

"We've got to wait," Mo'Steel said. "Jobs hates this stuff. We can't risk him bunnying out."

Too late. Billy and Mo'Steel were suddenly surrounded by a translucent substance. Mo'Steel felt the platform rocket into the air. The momentum knocked him to his knees.

Jobs hesitated. He met Violet's eyes and then shifted his gaze to Edward. His little brother's skin glowed with the same silvery light as the pyramid, making him hard to see.

Violet nodded, indicating she understood Jobs's unspoken plea. She'd watch out for Edward while he was gone. And if he didn't come back.

Jobs smiled his thanks. Then he ran after Mo'Steel, climbing the big steps, pushing himself to climb them quickly. Somehow he and Billy had to get control of the ship's computer, had to get control of Mother, before the Shipwright did.

Jobs knew it was impossible.

The Shipwright had a head start.

The Shipwright had operated the pyramid when they couldn't figure it out.

Jobs knew it was impossible.

He also knew they had to do it.

When he reached the top of the pyramid, he looked quickly around. Two of the raised platforms had been transformed into pillars that rose into the sky and out of sight.

Billy and Mo'Steel were gone.

Jobs felt his knees weaken, his stomach clench. He hated this heroic stuff. His stomach churned as he stepped onto the nearest platform.

Whoosh! Within seconds, he was airborne. Jobs fell to his hands and knees and threw up.

Tate had seen the expression on Tamara's face. Tamara was wandering, confused, lost. Tate was certain her connection with the Baby had been weakened or broken.

"Where are you going?" 2Face demanded.

Tate didn't have time to stop and have a big debate with 2Face. 2Face would never approve of what Tate was planning.

Kubrick was furious with indecision.

Should he follow the Shipwright? A fight was going to happen wherever Tamara, the Shipwright, Mo'Steel, and the others had gone. Kubrick wanted to be part of that fight. He wanted a piece of taking out the Shipwright.

The very sight of the alien made him so angry he could taste the bile on his tongue. Mother had turned him into a freak, trying to make him look more like the Shipwrights.

But what about 2Face? Kubrick glanced toward where she crouched, tensely watching the Riders and Blue Meanies. He couldn't leave her in the middle of a battle zone. He had to protect her. And besides, he hated the idea of being away from her.

He needed time to think!

Anamull nudged Kubrick and handed him the hoverboard Tate had left behind. "Take this," he said. "Get ready for an attack. Could be Meanies, could be Riders. It could even be Squids if any are still alive."

"Since when do I take orders from you?!" Kubrick demanded angrily.

"Not me — 2Face," Anamull said. "She told us to be prepared to fight."

Kubrick's chest loosened up. 2Face wanted him here. That decided it. He had to stay. He took the hoverboard from Anamull and nodded. "Thanks," he said. "I'll be ready."

CHAPTER TWENTY

"YOU HUMANS ARE TENACIOUS."

"Aaaaahhhhh!"

Mo'Steel let loose a goofy, wild-eyed yell.

This was no elevator. It was a rocket! Hard-core velocity firing straight up. So hard-core the G-force had pushed Billy and Mo'Steel down, down, down until they were lying flat on their backs staring up at the rapidly approaching sky. No, not a sky. The ceiling. The sky was only an illusion.

Mo'Steel's stomach was no longer cuddled snugly between his pelvis and ribs. He'd left it behind somewhere much closer to the ground.

A second passed. The ceiling raced closer. Mo'Steel wondered if they were going to crash into it.

Another second. Now Mo'Steel could see that the sky looked strange. Like a projection on a flat screen. Or a painting. Yes, more like blobs of pink paint on a white canvas. A painting that only makes sense when you are far, far away.

Another second. Mo'Steel closed his eyes and began to mumble a prayer, preparing to die, smashed like a bug. Then, miraculously, just in time, they began to slow. Mo'Steel felt the deceleration in his bones.

His skin began to tingle, starting with his scalp and moving rapidly down to his toes. He opened his eyes and found himself surrounded by a swirl of hazy colors that made him think of multicolored cotton candy.

The haze lifted. The rocket/elevator stopped. Mo'Steel and Billy scrambled to their feet and stepped off the platform.

Behind them, Jobs slowly rose into view. He was down on his hands and knees, head hanging, but he stood up woozily when his elevator stopped.

Tate appeared, looking relatively unscathed by the ride. Mo'Steel was surprised, but not unhappy, to see her. Tate struck him as brave and well-meaning. Not a bad sort to have along on their latest mission impossible.

The four of them gathered together, necks craned upward. They were in a baseball-stadium-size room. A transparent dome topped the walls towering high over their heads. Through the dome, Mo'Steel could see an immense array of twinkling stars.

"Anyone else feel underdressed?" Tate asked.

Mo'Steel nodded slowly. The place had a stark elegance, a cathedral-like solemnity that made the hairs on his arms stand at attention. He could almost imagine the Shipwrights meeting here for some sort of religious ritual.

The walls surrounding them were made of a smooth dull metal. Row after row of what looked almost like Egyptian hieroglyphics rose from the wall surfaces. Unlike hieroglyphics, though, these decorations were purely geometric — circles, squares, triangles, diamonds combined in endless variety.

"We are getting closer to Mother," Billy said.

Four archways, each several stories tall, opened off the space they were standing in. Long hallways lined with doors disappeared off into the distance. Some of the doors stood open, others were closed.

"It's so quiet and deserted," Tate said. "Almost like a Greek ruin."

"More like a haunted house with the furniture under slipcovers and the former inhabitants in the graveyard out back," Mo'Steel said.

"Thanks for that image," Jobs said.

Mo'Steel shrugged. "What now?"

"We explore," Jobs said. "One of these doors has to lead to Mother." He started down the closest of the hallways. Mo'Steel moved to follow when something made him turn around. He was just in time to see Tamara and the Shipwright come out into the hallway directly behind them. Tamara hardly seemed to notice that they were there. Her attention was riveted on the Shipwright.

"You humans are tenacious." Mo'Steel saw the Shipwright's opaque head vibrate and heard an echoing voice in his head. Somehow the mouthless Shipwright was talking. "Perhaps that is an admirable quality."

Something about that "perhaps" made Mo'Steel's skin crawl.

Tate searched Tamara's face for some hint of recognition, for some sparkle of humanity. Her face was cold and empty, her eyes hard. Still, Tate noticed that Tamara's movements seemed to be her own. She wasn't moving in sync with the Shipwright in the way she often did with the Baby.

There was hope.

"I have work to do," the Shipwright said. "You

must leave." The Shipwright's words were toneless, but its impatience was clear enough.

Tate glanced at Jobs, Mo'Steel, Billy. None of them made a move to go. The boys had come to fight for control of the bridge. She'd come to free Tamara. They couldn't give up so easily.

"Do not worry," the Shipwright said. "I will let you live. I will see after your care. Mother is vast. There is plenty of room for all."

Billy's face was dark with anger. What did he know? Tate could only guess. Mo'Steel was looking to Jobs. But Jobs looked like a speeder who's just seen a state trooper in his rearview mirror.

Well, Tate, for one, wasn't willing to let an opportunity to talk to the Baby/Shipwright pass. "Why would you want to take care of us?" she asked.

The Shipwright turned to her. Tate felt her bowels go liquid but she held her ground.

"You interest me," the Shipwright said. "Why would I destroy such an interesting species? Entertainment is hard to find in the universe."

"You didn't seem to have any problem ordering the destruction of the Blue Meanies," Tate said. "And they seem pretty interesting to me. Those fighting wings? Good stuff."

"I will decide what interests me," the Shipwright said.

"What interests you is control," Tate said. "Control over Mother. Same as the Blue Meanies. That's why you want them out of the way."

Tate felt as if there was no going back now. She surprised herself by taking a step closer to the Shipwright. "There are only two reasons why you'd let us live," she said. "Either you think we're no threat. Or you're afraid of us."

"Afraid of humans?" the Shipwright said.

"Afraid of one of us," Tate said.

She turned her gaze to Billy.

Humans.

A most perplexing species.

They were emotional, lost, unarmed.

They were at a tactical disadvantage they could never overcome.

They were too few in number to maintain a healthy biological sample.

They were religious, superstitious, primitive.

And yet they possessed intelligence, tenacity, intuition. Intuition most of all. How could this female guess the Makers feared the Deviant? She could not know the powers he possessed. Could not know how rare his gift was. Could not know what he was capable of destroying, of creating.

He was called Te. And the female dared challenge him.

Dared call Te a coward.

It was an insult!

It was an opening.

A chance to destroy the Deviant now. Now, before he discovered the extent of his own abilities.

Te reached out for his weapon, for the one who followed his like a lovesick *mnok,* for the human called Tamara. Te ordered her to kill and launched her at the Deviant.

CHAPTER TWENTY-ONE

"MAKE YOUR LAST PRAYER A SHORT ONE."

Stop Tamara.

Mo'Steel heard the command and was leaping toward the Marine sergeant before he had time to wonder who was talking in his head. Leaping like a highly caffeinated gazelle and landing eight feet from where he took off. Mo'Steel blinked in surprise.

How?

Tamara was right in front of him.

Mo'Steel twisted ninety degrees and aimed his right heel at her throat. She shifted back, inviting him to knock himself over with his momentum.

Not a chance. He bounced forward onto his right foot, twisted to the left, and landed a solid kick to her chest. He was a ninja warrior. He was a freaking Crouching Dragon.

"Mo! Don't be stupid!" Jobs yelled.

Tamara came at him, her fists a blur.

Mo'Steel kicked off, back flipped, and landed with his fists at the ready.

How?

He'd never studied martial arts. He wasn't even much of a fighter. Sure, he'd fight to defend himself or protect a friend. But that hadn't been necessary too often. He wasn't small enough to be bully bait. And, in general, people liked him.

He certainly had no desire to fight Tamara Hoyle. She was a trained Marine, not to mention possessed by an alien capable of turning her into a killing machine.

Tamara came forward swinging.

Mo'Steel held his hands out like a traffic cop, stopping her volley of punches with his palms. *Thwack, thwack. Thwackthwackthwack.* Her hands moved faster than he could see and yet somehow he anticipated her actions. He was superhuman. Like Billy.

That was it.

Billy.

Billy was whispering in his brain. Billy was moving his muscles. Mo'Steel felt a rush of resentment, a repulsion. He was no one's puppet! Billy couldn't pull his strings the way the Shipwright pulled Tamara's.

But that was stupid. Billy was a friend. He'd saved Mo'Steel's life, saved his mother's life. If he needed Mo'Steel to hold off Tamara, then, well, Mo'Steel just hoped he didn't get killed in the process.

Mo'Steel breathed deeply, opened himself up, and felt a surge of power like nothing he had ever imagined. Billy's whisper turned into a shout.

Tamara's fists were still moving. And, in the middle of that, Mo'Steel was still able to turn his head and watch as the Shipwright moved down a hallway and slipped through a door. Billy looked at Mo'Steel for a long moment and then followed the Shipwright.

"Mo!" Jobs yelled. "I'm going after Billy."

"Cool," Mo'Steel said, keeping his eyes on Tamara. "I got this under control."

Tamara spun away from him. When she spun back, she was holding a weapon. A short, featureless tube. She took aim and squeezed a trigger.

Fléchettes!

They zoomed toward Mo'Steel — a thousand pieces of razor-sharp metal flying toward his face, his body. Mo'Steel leaned way, way back, limboing, bending from his ankles, and watched the fléchettes pass overhead like a swarm of irate wasps. When the firing stopped, Mo'Steel stood up again, amazed, feeling like Gumby.

"Aaaaahhhh!" Mo'Steel yelled, an expression of joy.

A flash of movement behind a door. Tate, taking shelter.

Tamara threw down the fléchette gun. She pulled a spear from the Rider bandolier she wore across her chest and charged.

Down a hallway! Mo'Steel ran faster than he'd ever run before. Yet he could hear Tamara's level breathing behind him.

Closer, closer.

Mo'Steel yanked open a door, dashed inside. Tamara was right behind him. Mo'Steel glanced around, getting his bearings, searching for a weapon.

Rows of shelves lined with pint-size containers made of something like glass. Tables. Gleaming robotic equipment. The smell of rotting fish.

A laboratory?

Mo'Steel wedged himself between one of the shelves and the wall. She moved in front of the shelves, jabbing at Mo'Steel between the rows of glasslike containers.

What was with the jars? They contained liquids of different colors. Murky shapes. Something that looked like a Rider's insect eye. No time to worry about that now.

"Timber," Mo'Steel whispered to himself.

He pushed.

The shelf tilted toward Tamara, the glasslike containers rocking, and then crashed over. Hundreds of containers shattered. Something like acid sizzled. Unidentifiable lumps of something slithered out onto the floor. An unbearable reek of something foul and rotten filled the air.

Mo'Steel gagged, ran.

The shelf rose up and crashed over the other way.

Tamara jumped up, looking incredibly ticked off, still holding her spear.

Mo'Steel backed up, fighting for air.

Tamara leaped at him. She was inches from landing on his shoulders when he crouched, did a back somersault, came to his feet, let out a whoop of delight, stepped forward, stuck his foot out, and tripped Tamara. She fell forward, hitting her head on the edge of a counter with an audible thunk. Tamara slid to the floor, eyes closed, dazed. Her knees crumpled under her.

"I think she's out," Tate said quietly. She was standing in the doorway, covering her nose and mouth with her hand.

Mo'Steel nodded, turned for a second to smile at Tate.

Tamara pounced. She grabbed Mo'Steel's head in two strong hands and smiled down at him. "Make your last prayer a short one," she said. "One good twist and you're gone."

"No!" Tate yelled.

Mo'Steel saw a shadow of uncertainty pass across Tamara's face. Her grip faltered and he rolled free.

Tate took a gingerly step toward Tamara. "You can fight the Shipwright's control," she whispered.

Tamara reached a hand out to Tate.

Tate stepped forward to take it.

And then Tate flew backward and slammed into a wall. "Don't you ever shut up?" Tamara asked.

CHAPTER TWENTY-TWO

"THAT BIG STARFISH IS SCARED OF YOU."

With a small part of his mind, Billy powered Mo'Steel. Fed him energy to fight. Fueled his muscles. Heightened his senses.

Meanwhile, his body followed the Shipwright through a vast maze. Room after room. Each one different. Billy amused himself by guessing at their functions: laboratory, theater, kitchen. Did the Shipwrights eat even though they didn't have mouths? Or had they evolved beyond the need for food?

The Shipwright moved purposefully, swiftly through the rooms. The alien made no sign that it was aware of Billy's presence or bothered by him.

Billy wondered why the alien was in such a hurry. He reached out for the Shipwright's brain. For a moment, he was lost, probing in the darkness.

Then —

His mind connected with the alien consciousness.

The Shipwright's brain was shaped like a skinny star, radiating out from a center point into the alien's limbs and head. The tissue wasn't gray like a human brain. No, it was a beautiful, glittering pink, like fiber-optic cable. Impulses moved along its extensive, straight pathways a thousand times faster than any human had ever thought.

But Billy could follow the movements. Could sense the Shipwright's mood. Something like . . .

Impatience.

Uncertainty.

Not exactly the same as human emotions, but close enough. Recognizable. The Shipwright didn't want to spend time dealing with Billy. The fight between Tamara and Mo'Steel was already enough of a distraction.

The Shipwright, startled, turned swiftly toward Billy. The alien had sensed his probing. "Don't make me destroy you," the Shipwright said.

Billy made no reply. The emotions were coming in faster, clearer now.

Worry.

Hesitation.

Fear.

The Shipwright was afraid of him. Billy didn't know why, couldn't guess how he could harm the Shipwright. He only knew that he could.

They reached a door that dwarfed the others they had passed.

"Do not follow me," the Shipwright warned.

The Shipwright opened the immense door and stepped into the room beyond.

Billy followed. He found himself in a massive open space. The room was octagonal. Dozens of the strangely proportioned, padded Shipwright chairs lined the walls. The chairs were a kind of computer interface. Billy had sat in one to communicate with Mother.

The Shipwright was moving down the row of chairs, pausing to place a hand on each seat before moving on.

The ceiling was a giant screen that showed the space they were passing through. Stars glittered in the distance. Smaller screens seemed to be showing the environments below them. Billy could see the ruins of the battlefield. A few Meanies and the Riders fought on.

The bridge.

Billy moved toward one of the chairs. This was

his opportunity to connect with Mother, to gain control of the ship for his friends.

But before he could sit down, the Shipwright materialized in front of him. Anger radiated from it. Anger and something else.

Fear.

They stared at each other silently.

Jobs ran through the door. Stopped when he saw them.

Billy felt the air go out of his lungs. He was knocked backward like a rag doll, even though nothing had touched him. The Shipwright had attacked. Not with his stumpy arms. With his mind.

Violet's stomach was twisted with worry. The pain got worse with every second that ticked by.

What would happen if Jobs, Mo'Steel, and the others never came back? How long should they wait? Where would they go?

Anamull and Kubrick were standing guard, reminding Violet of little boys playing cowboys and Indians. What could they do against an army of aliens? Edward inched as close to the older boys as he dared, clearly longing to get into the game.

D-Caf and Yago were huddled together, discussing who knew what. Yago seemed to be doing most of the talking. Burroway and T.R. had separated themselves somewhat from the rest of the group. 2Face's attention was focused on the endless bloody battle, perhaps trying to gauge who would win. Noyze, Dr. Cohen, and Olga were turned the other way — watching the top of the pyramid and waiting for Mo'Steel and the others to return.

"Rider!" Edward yelled.

The Rider was alone, but there was no mistaking his attentions. He was pushing his hoverboard to top speed, and his spear was pointing at them.

"But we're supposed to be on their side," Burroway complained. "Tamara said we'd be safe as long as we stayed out of the way."

"Yeah, well, Tamara isn't here," Kubrick said. "Get back."

Violet scrambled to her feet and pulled Edward back. He twisted impatiently under her touch.

The Rider let out a high-pitched war cry that made Violet shudder.

Anamull laughed, mounted his board, and raced out to meet the Rider. Kubrick briefly glanced at 2Face and then followed.

Violet wanted to tell Edward not to look. He

had seen enough pain, suffering, and death for a little boy. But Violet knew Edward would resent being treated like a kid.

Instead, she lowered her own gaze and fought the urge to plug her ears. She didn't want to see any more of the Remnants killed.

Tate opened her eyes and stared senselessly at the edge of a table. She felt herself breathe in, breathe out. Her chest hurt. Her back hurt. Her head hurt. Where was she?

A grunt somewhere close by.

Tate shifted slightly and watched unbelievingly as Mo'Steel ran straight up a wall and hopped onto the top of a huge machine. He crouched there, throwing some sort of tools down at Tamara, waiting for her to follow him. Tamara began scaling the machine like a rock climber.

Feeling totally defeated, Tate closed her eyes again.

For a long, long moment Billy lay motionless on the ground.

Jobs, sick at heart, weak-kneed, keeping one eye on the Shipwright, staggered to his friend's side. "Billy? Billy, can you hear me?"

Billy lifted his head and gazed sadly at Jobs. He looked like a scared, sick, skinny orphan.

Then, without moving, without touching Billy, the Shipwright attacked again. Billy clutched at his own throat, struggling for air. Struggling — and losing.

Jobs watched, helpless, as Billy's face turned a brilliant red and then shaded toward blue-gray. His eyes, protruding strangely out of his skull, focused on Jobs with a silent plea.

"Stop it!" Jobs yelled. "Stop it! You'll kill him!"

The Shipwright was already turning away, moving back toward the chairs. Jobs was invisible to the alien. Unimportant. So why had the Shipwright taken the energy to kill Billy? Tate had to be right. Billy was important to the Shipwright. Dangerous, even.

Jobs turned back to Billy. "Fight him!" he sobbed desperately. "That big starfish is scared of you. Can't you feel it?"

Billy closed his eyes.

Jobs could hear his own heart beating.

Beat, beat, beat, beat.

Billy took a sudden breath. A deep, shuddering breath that shook his entire body. He sat up. And now the Shipwright was clutching its milky head with two four-fingered hands.

"That's it," Jobs whispered, backing away. "Fight it. You can do it."

The Shipwright seemed to break free of Billy's psychic grip. Slowly, Billy got to his feet and the two approached each other. Jobs watched as they circled, each taking the measure of his opponent.

"Humans," the Maker said. "Te has called you tenacious. But there is a better word in your primitive language. *Suicidal.* Only a creature that wished to die would challenge a Maker on its own ship, in a world it helped create."

Billy said nothing. Just kept circling.

Three feet from Jobs was a plasma screen, or the Shipwright's version of a plasma screen. Along the edges were rows of the omnipresent geometric shapes — a miniature version of the frieze on the pyramid. A keyboard. Or something close to it.

Keeping one eye on Billy and the Shipwright, Jobs eased closer to the keyboard. The Shipwright didn't react. It was still taunting Billy.

"Even if you destroy me, what do you hope to accomplish, human?" the Shipwright asked. "You will never control Mother. Mother is in collapse. Only I can save her. Only I can save this ship."

Jobs smiled to himself. The Shipwright sounded

awfully sure of itself, but Jobs had a feeling it was bluffing. If Billy could buy him enough time, he could hack into Mother. Jobs took another step forward and ran his fingers lightly over the keyboard.

All he needed was a little time.

CHAPTER TWENTY-THREE

"JUST A LITTLE MORE TIME."

Insanity.

Schizophrenia.

Billy's mind was in two places at once. Helping Mo'Steel fight Tamara. Keeping the Shipwright from killing him.

He was playing two deadly chess games at once. If his concentration on Mo'Steel faltered, his friend would die. If he gave Mo'Steel too much attention, he would die himself and that, too, would equal Mo'Steel's death.

So he helped Mo'Steel anticipate a rapid sequence of kicks from Tamara. And, at the same time, he followed the Shipwright — Te — onto a battlefield that existed only in an infinite, unreal dream-space where their two minds had agreed to meet.

Flat black ground and white sky. A bare canvas

that could become anything they had the strength to imagine.

Billy and Te were without weapons.

They would fight only with the power of their minds.

They stood facing each other. Billy's battered sneakers toe-to-toe with the Shipwright's naked birdlike feet.

Billy felt a sudden crippling pain in his feet, his calves. A pain so intense he cried out, nearly wet his pants. He looked down and saw pea-green worms burrowing through his flesh.

No!

This wasn't real.

Billy feverishly told himself he wasn't really in this dream-space. The pain was only as real as he allowed it to be. He forced himself to ignore the agony, to imagine his legs whole and healthy. He willed the worms to disappear. Then he turned his torment into energy. He shot a lightning bolt out of his finger, nailing Te in his chest.

The Shipwright staggered backward, transparent skin glowing from the intense burst of electricity.

A pause. Billy breathed deeply. Rested. Sent another surge of energy to Mo'Steel.

Another mind swarmed into his consciousness. A vision of Jobs floated up into the dream-space. Jobs hunched over one of Mother's tactical interfaces, his mind buzzing with excitement.

No time for Jobs.

Concentrate. Concentrate on his two opponents, Tamara and Te. Concentrate on —

Something falling from the sky! Something metallic and covered in glittering points. A bomb! It hit just in front of Billy and exploded. He was airborne, flying backward, feeling the shards of metal. He landed hard. For a moment — searing pain in his shoulder, his legs.

Then Billy laughed it off.

That was the best bomb the Shipwrights had created? When it came to destruction, humans were far more advanced. He dug into the history of Earth and brought an image into his mind. An ancient image, from a war that had ended more than sixty years before Billy was born. The Shipwright looked up and saw what seemed to be a primitive bomb falling toward it.

The alien instantly surrounded itself by what looked like a protective bubble made of a translucent goo.

A blinding flash!

Dead silence. Then —

BOOM!

The Shipwright and its bubble were obliterated by a fireball rising and churning within itself. The fireball gave rise to a mushroom cloud that towered tens of thousands of feet into the air.

A series of shock waves knocked Billy to his feet. But only seconds passed before the Shipwright came crawling away from the fire. It was weak, its see-through skin marred by soot.

Attack! Attack! Billy told himself.

But Billy was distracted by Mo'Steel. Over-whelmed by the vivid image of Mo'Steel leaping across a body of water. Leaping so far he was almost airborne. Tamara was right behind him. Billy helped Mo'Steel change directions in midair, flipping over Tamara so that she became the hunted and Mo'Steel the hunter.

Billy imagined a steel box. A small steel box with the Shipwright stuffed inside. But Te was fighting him. Te's star-shaped mind was racing.

Excitement.

Billy turned, stared.

An old woman was wandering across the empty

dream-space. She was hunched over, feeble. Billy felt his heart miss as she moved closer. Could she be a weapon? Should he destroy her? Yes! Only . . .

What kind of weapon was this?

The woman had a human head. A head that greatly resembled his adoptive mother, Jessica. She was wearing a warm-up suit. But the arms and legs were too short. The four-fingered hands and bird-like feet of a Shipwright poked out of the arms and legs.

She wasn't a weapon.

She was an embodiment of Mother.

Billy knew it.

And he knew the Maker knew it.

Jobs jumped back. The keyboard he'd been tapping had suddenly lit up and was glowing with a soft red light. The plasma screen in front of him whirled and hummed as it came to life.

Jobs glanced nervously over his shoulder. Had the Shipwright noticed? No. No, the Shipwright and Billy stood silently, still as stone. Only Billy's eyes moved, jerking rapidly beneath his closed lids.

"Just a little more time," Jobs muttered to himself.

CHAPTER TWENTY-FOUR

"NO FALSE MOVES."

The Shipwright was on its birdlike feet, racing toward Mother.

Billy blinked, understood what was happening, and began to run after Te. This may have been only an embodiment of Mother, but it was a way to control her. She was offering herself up. The only question was: To whom?

Te was closing in, quickly drawing closer to the little old woman who represented the humans' best chance for survival. Billy pushed his muscles as hard as he could, but Te was faster, much faster. Perhaps that was because Mother was helping it, because Mother wanted Te to win.

Then, suddenly, Billy ran into something, something very solid. He stepped back, clutching his nose. He looked up — way up — at a stone wall. The wall was very high and seemed to stretch from horizon to horizon.

Te was on the other side.

So was Mother.

Billy stretched his arms out and pressed his body against the wall.

He'd lost.

"A firewall," Jobs muttered angrily.

Of course, that wasn't it exactly. The block Mother had created was far more elaborate, subtle, and sophisticated than anything the most creative programmer on Earth had ever dreamed into being.

Jobs had to erase it.

He had to get rid of the block before the Shipwright killed Billy.

Jobs's hands were shaking; his body was slick with cold sweat. He was breathing in shallow gasps. He closed his eyes and tried to take a deep breath. Nothing doing. His chest was in a vise grip screwed down tight.

One false move and Mother would lock him out of the system forever. One miss and what remained of humanity would live out their lives as slaves of the Shipwrights or worse.

"Okay, then," Jobs muttered to himself. "No false moves." His fingers began to move over the keyboard.

Creaking.

Groaning.

A shudder moved through the wall.

Billy stepped back, looked up. A crack was growing in the massive fortress. Far, far overhead a stone the size of a dump truck wiggled loose and began to fall a thousand feet from the top of the wall.

"Ahhhh!" Billy called out.

He ran, stumbling in his panic. The stone hit the ground with a tremendous impact. Billy fell, scrambled to his feet, ran again. Another stone hit and knocked him down.

Billy glanced backward and gasped when he saw that the stones weren't falling randomly. They were forming a crude stairway with each step nearly as tall as Billy. He changed direction, crossed the distance to the first stone, put his hands on top, and pulled himself up. Then the next stone. Billy kept going, climbing five or six stories, until he could see over the partially crumbled wall.

The old woman — Mother — stood in the middle of the vast white plain. The Shipwright was grabbing at her, trying to force her down onto the ground. She struggled, crying out, beating the alien off with weak slaps and kicks.

There was no way down.

No staircase led to the other side of the wall. Billy was trapped on the edge, seventy feet in the air. Stretching his hands out toward Mother, he let out a scream of frustration that echoed back at him.

He had to stop the Shipwright.

Even if it meant his own death.

Even if it meant Mo'Steel's.

Tears flowing, Billy expanded his mind. He let go of Mo'Steel. He let go of Jobs. He reached out for Mother with every fiber, forgetting everything else.

Mother cried out, her own scream an exact duplicate of Billy's. The old woman dissolved into a whirlwind that slipped through the Shipwright's grasp. Spinning furiously toward Billy, moving with blinding speed, the whirlwind crossed the dreamscape and disappeared into Billy's screaming mouth.

Billy shuddered violently. Foam formed in the corners of his mouth. Jobs turned from the keyboard, his attention split between the computer and his friend. Should he keep working? Or could he do something to help Billy?

Jobs didn't dare leave the computer. Billy seemed to be losing his battle. Jobs was worried he might have only a few more seconds to hack into Mother.

"Billy!" Jobs yelled. "Are you okay?"

"Yes." Billy spoke without moving, making Jobs wonder if he was hearing things.

Jobs looked down at his shaking hands. The keyboard's red glow had been replaced by a blue one. Jobs wasn't sure what the change meant, but he knew it was major.

The dream-scape disappeared. Billy was aware of himself standing sneaker-to-feet with the Shipwright on the bridge. The alien looked exactly the same, but its mind felt different. Its fear was so strong Billy could taste it.

Fear of Billy.

Fear of failing his people.

Fear of death.

"You are not human," the Shipwright said.

Billy could sense Jobs's thoughts bubbling up: interest, curiosity, repulsion. His fingers rested on the alien keyboard, but he was concentrating on Billy and the Shipwright.

"I am human," Billy said.

A memory flashed in his mind. For an instant, it

was vivid and powerful. Then it receded into the mists, leaving Billy with only shadowy images. Shapes surrounding him. A field of energy pulsating.

What did the memory mean?

Billy shook it off. It meant nothing! It was nothing but a remembered hallucination.

But why was it so vague?

Billy's memories were always clear. Even the things that hadn't happened to him were clear. He could remember the cloying smell of fresh soil in the hole where Yago had spent a terrifying night. The wet sound of Kubrick's skin separating from his muscle. Billy could see these and a billion more vivid details. So why was this one memory so fuzzy?

"Something is happening to the Shipwright!"

Jobs. Sounding amazed and terrified.

Yes. The racing pulses of its brain were slowing. Even the taste of its fear was fading.

"The ancient enemy," the Shipwright said. Then the pulses stopped. The taste disappeared.

Billy's knees gave out. Exhaustion hit him like a hammer to the skull. He sat down hard with barely the energy to breathe, to keep his heart beating.

Jobs appeared at his side. "Is it gone?"

Billy nodded, depressed by his victory. Yes, the

Shipwright whose ancestors had created this ship was gone. The humans had prevailed over their environment once again.

"Can you get up?" Jobs asked.

Billy did a mental check and found strength pouring into his muscles, his bloodstream, his cells.

He stood up.

CHAPTER TWENTY-FIVE

"JUST NAPPING."

"Kick!" Mo'Steel commanded his legs.

The only response was a feeble twitch. The strange, wonderful, superhuman power had drained out of him. Mo'Steel felt its loss desperately. No more incredible leaps. No more clinging to the walls.

And besides, now it was all over.

Tamara towered over him. Then, suddenly, her eyes rolled back in her head and she slumped forward, landing half on top of him.

Was she dead?

Excited, scared, disgusted, Mo'Steel used the last of his energy to push her off him. She was still alive. Her eyelids fluttered.

Tate came running. She looked into Mo'Steel's eyes, then bent to examine Tamara.

"Her pulse is faint," Tate said, her brow wrinkled with worry. "Are you okay?"

"Tired," Mo'Steel said. "Thirsty."

Tate reached over and gave him an impulsive hug. "I'm so glad you're alive! Both of you. I thought . . ."

"Yeah," Mo'Steel said. "Me, too."

Billy and Jobs emerged from one of the rooms. They came down the hallway toward the others. Mo'Steel thought Billy looked different. Bigger almost. More powerful. Jobs followed half a step behind him.

Mo'Steel pulled himself to his knees. Tate helped him to his feet. He felt as if he had just powered through three back-to-back quadathlons. Every muscle, every joint, every bone ached.

"Mo!" Jobs yelled. "You don't look too good."

"You should see the other guy," Mo'Steel mumbled.

Jobs eyed Tamara. "Is she dead?"

Mo'Steel shook his head, making himself see stars. "Nah. Just napping. What happened to the Shipwright?"

Jobs glanced at Billy. "They had a fight."

"And?" Tate demanded.

"Billy won," Jobs said.

Billy met Tate's gaze. "Tamara is free."

Tate swallowed hard and nodded numbly, tears in her eyes.

"I need to go downstairs," Billy said. He started toward the elevator.

"I'll stay here with Tamara," Tate said.

Mo'Steel nodded, fell into step next to Jobs. The three boys stepped onto one platform. The platform glowed with life and they began to descend slowly.

"Nice ride," Mo'Steel said, smiling at Billy. "Smooth."

Jobs grinned, too. "Yeah, I don't even feel like puking. Of course, my stomach is empty from the ride up."

The corners of Billy's mouth twitched upward, but his gaze was distant. Mo'Steel felt suddenly uneasy about what was going to happen when they reached the environment. The fact that Billy looked so gloomy couldn't be a good sign. Billy had beaten the Shipwright. They should be celebrating.

"Hey, 'migo, you okay?" Mo'Steel asked Billy.

Billy studied him for a moment before speaking. "Mo, do you think I'm human?"

Mo'Steel barked out a nervous laugh. Shot a

worried look at Jobs. "Sure you're human," he said. "What else would you be?"

"I — I don't know."

The platform came to a rest. The boys stepped off.

"Romeo!" Olga shouted.

Mo'Steel went to his mother, gave her a hug. Violet, 2Face, and Edward surrounded Jobs. He told them about the Shipwright. The babble of voices rose as the others questioned Jobs, tried to figure out what this latest development meant for them.

"What happened to you?" Olga demanded urgently. "You're shaking. Your clothes are soaked. Are you okay?"

"Fine," Mo'Steel said. And, actually, he was starting to feel better. Still thirsty, though. "Everyone here okay?"

"A Rider attacked us," Olga reported shakily. "Anamull is wounded. A stab wound on his leg. Nothing serious. All of the rest of us are fine. I guess."

Mo'Steel looked out onto the battlefield. Amazingly, sadly, the battle still raged.

The Meanies had apparently regrouped and renewed their attack after the Shipwright disappeared. The Riders still shouted their piercing war cry, but now they sounded hoarse and weary. Their hoverboards moved over the bodies of their enemies and their Clansmen as they continued to throw spears and boomerangs skyward.

Billy climbed the steps of the pyramid. While the others stared up at him in disbelief, Billy faced the battlefield and raised his arms in the air.

"Stop this!" he yelled.

"We have to stop him," Olga said urgently. "They'll kill him. Billy, get down!"

Mo'Steel held his mother back. "Wait. I think it's okay."

In a way, Mo'Steel was right. None of the Meanies or Riders attacked Billy. But they also didn't stop fighting.

Billy drew his arms to his chest and closed his eyes.

The Rider environment vanished. The hills, the coppery ocean, the strange spastic trees, the pink sky all disappeared. In their place appeared two towering stone walls. The pyramid, the battlefield, the Meanies, the Riders, and the humans were all contained within the space between the two walls.

That got the Riders' and the Meanies' attention.

Meanies circled without firing. Riders' weapons dropped at their sides as they turned to stare at Billy. Mo'Steel, Olga, and the other Remnants stared, too.

Billy stood on the top of the pyramid. He held his arms wide, holding up the walls with the strength of his mind. The threat was unspoken but clear. Time to listen or get splattered.

"Enough fighting," Billy commanded.

With that, the battle ended.

The Riders dropped their boomerangs and spears. They rode their hoverboards in confused circles, gradually coalescing in a worried little knot.

Withdrawing their cutting wings, the Blue Meanies landed together in a small huddle, tentacles waving furiously.

The humans, too, drew together.

Mo'Steel tore his eyes from Billy to study the faces around him. Noyze and Dr. Cohen were exchanging brilliant smiles of pure relief. Violet and Jobs stood together, their fingers barely touching, eyes wide, jaws slack. Awed. Kubrick looked disappointed. No doubt he hated to see a good fight end.

2Face glanced toward Mo'Steel. Her dark eyes were cold with something very much like hatred.

*   *   *

This was not the Path.

Yago was destined to destroy Tamara. He and his loyal supporters. Not Billy. Not a freak.

Yago could not stand it. He could not have others competing with him.

He was the One.

The only One.

Billy would have to be destroyed.

K.A. APPLEGATE

REMNANTS™

⑧

Mother, May I?

"I've found something, Violet," Jobs told her. Told her that he'd shown the lumpish mass to Mo'Steel, that Mo'Steel agreed it looked an awful lot like the remains of planet Earth and its moon.

Violet took the news with little expression of interest.

"Isn't it exciting?" Jobs said, puzzled by her indifference.

"I don't know what to say, Jobs," she admitted. "I don't see what good it does us now to have found — Earth. Or what's left of it. It just sounds very, very sad, to me. I'm sorry."

Jobs shook his head. "But don't you see, Violet? There's a chance, slim but a chance, that Earth's still habitable. That we could go back and with Billy's help and the ship's resources, maybe, just maybe, the human race could be independent again. Owners and not renters. We could start over and —"

Violet laughed but her eyes were sad. "Oh, Jobs, you're deluded. Forget what you saw, or think you saw. Pursuing this is only going to break your heart."

Jobs ran his hand through his already unruly hair. He suddenly remembered his mother calling him Egg-Beater Head. Back on Earth. Back home.

He had to make Violet understand.

"Honestly, Violet," he said, "can you really just let this go? Don't you want to go and see what might be the remains of Earth, see where it takes us? Can you really just forget about it, just turn away, go on living aboard Mother for the duration? Not knowing if she'll ever decide she doesn't want us here anymore. Never knowing what might have been on Earth."

"I want to stay," Violet said immediately, almost angrily. "It's safer. Smarter. Look, what if the planet *is* Earth? What then? Maybe it's not habitable. Probably it's not. What if Billy can't fix it all for us? I don't want another disappointment like that. I don't need to lose my home twice in one lifetime." Violet shook her head. "One very long lifetime."

"But this is not really your home," Jobs argued

"It is now. It is because I've chosen it to be and I've accepted its limitations. All of them. No, Jobs. I don't want to leave."

"You're afraid."

Violet smiled. "That's what I've been saying."

"But what if — just what if — the planet is Earth and it is habitable and we can rebuild —"

"What? Rebuild what, Jobs? A fabulous civilization, just like that? With a handful of people, most of whom, excuse me for being blunt, are selfish and cowardly and who can't even agree on what an extra-cheese taco should taste like?"

Jobs sighed. "But what if we can go home, Violet? Just use your imagination, okay? Please?"

Violet took Jobs's hands, looked into his eyes. Her own were dark. "Jobs, I miss Earth so badly," she said, her voice breaking. "I try not to think about the past but I can't help it. I dream about it almost every night. How could I not? I'm homesick. Sometimes the nostalgia is so piercing I think I'm going to die, just fall to the floor and die with longing. How can I try to go back to something I know is no longer there? How can I avoid hoping, futilely, I know, but hoping that something, any little thing will be the same as it was five hundred years ago? When nothing is the same. Nothing."

"Aren't you the least bit curious, though?" Jobs persisted. "Because maybe something good did remain. Maybe, I don't know, some trees. Maybe some people. Violet, it's unlikely, but there could be people alive on that planet. Humans."

"Humans?" Violet laughed harshly and pulled her hands from his. "No, Jobs. More like descendants of a few wrecked survivors of the greatest catastrophe our world has ever known. What could we possibly have in common with them? They're probably like a different species now! They might be without a spoken language, without writing, without machines, without the wheel for all we know! Jobs, they might not even be breathing oxygen! I'm not saying they're worthless. I'm saying they're not us. The human race as we know it consists of a handful of relics on board a massive space ship. That's all."

Jobs felt defeated. "Maybe the Missing Eight are there," he suggested lamely.

Violet just looked at him.

"Will you go along if the others choose to?" he said after a moment.

"I'm a captive to the will of the people, Jobs," Violet said. She sounded resigned. "Aren't I?"

"Aren't we all," Jobs said wearily.

Light-Years From Home...And On Their Own

REMNANTS
K.A. Applegate